The Werewolf charged...

Raising his spear, Geoffrey Turner caught the beast full in its hirsute chest with the barbed prongs. Hardly fazed, the furious nightcreature slashed with its claws.

Oliver saw no hope for the man Turner. Or for himself. Then Turner flipped a switch on the spear. There was a buzzing. The werewolf howled. Wisps of gray smoke rose from its chest and face. The animal dropped to the road.

"Magical, sir!" Oliver breathed. "And you, sir, must be a magician. Or sorcerer, even."

"Tut tut. Nothing of the sort. I want you to have a closer look at our dead friend here."

Oliver gasped. Instead of burned flesh and singed fur, he saw the gleam of metal, lengths of discolored wiring.

"An android," explained Turner, "Part flesh, part robot. They're all this way. Always have been. The werewolves, the dragons, even the vampires. And controlling them all is a computer."

But behind the computer was a human being, the most heinous of all—and he had to be destroyed . . .

D1008073

NIGHTWORLD

David Bischoff

A Del Rey Book

BALLANTINE BOOKS • NEW YORK

A Del Rey Book
Published by Ballantine Books

Library of Congress Catalog Card Number: 78-61853

ISBN 0-345-27605-1

Manufactured in the United States of America

First Edition: January 1979

For the Falstaff and Poins
of my science fiction youth,
Richard and Robert Reiter

With special thanks to
Judy-Lynn del Rey
Owen Lock
Henry Morrison . . .
and
Ray Harryhausen, for
Special effects inspiration.

PROLOGUE

━━━━━━━━━━━━━━━━━━━━━━

   The sun set and moonless, cloudy night poured across the land.

   The vampire awoke.

   Nestled comfortably in a satin-lined coffin, the creature felt the Summons immediately. It raised the coffin lid, hesitated briefly and looked about, then stepped out onto the chill flags of the chapel floor. The vampire answered with its mind: "Master—I come."

   As it stepped into the Nightworld, the creature pondered the Summons. Satan had not called for months. True, the Master had other Servants. Multitudes. But the proximity of its crypt and its admirable record often caused Satan to employ the vampire on missions of considerable import.

   Evidently, one such task awaited.

   The soft whisper of silk against silk; the black of the creature's clothes echoed the wind and night curling around the forest's shivering leaves. Save for the deep crimson of its lips, pallor clung to the exposed surfaces of the beast's face and hands like a brittle sheath of

1

new-fallen snow. The nostrils of its aquiline nose were wide to the scents of the night: the comforting stench of the dead, the seductive fragrance of the living. The eyes owned no color at all, twin windows into oblivion. Its lips were parted, and between lay a darkness marred only by two white points.

Though the night was chill, its breath did not mist.

Walking slowly through the graveyard, long black cape billowing behind, it recalled the way. The path to Hell was not an easy one, and remembering the proper code for the Gates was important. Most important.

Mist already covered the ground and obscured the undergrowth as the vampire gained the forest. Wolves howled to the east and a loud thrashing paralleled his path through the dark trees. Another time the vampire might have investigated. But not that night.

After a time, a mottled moon rose, and a pale shimmer leaked from a break in the roiling clouds. Awakened by the gleam, bats flapped toward the fitfully illumined mountain in the near-distance.

The vampire turned in the same direction, for at the base of the mountain lay the Gates.

They gleamed with silver fire as the vampire approached and slipped its identification card into the appropriate slot. With a sharp-nailed finger, it tapped the combination.

A voice erupted from the speaker grille . . .

"Guardian Nine Oh Six Aye Four," it said in an emotionless monotone. "You are expected, Vampire Four Nine Bee Oh Oh. The Master awaits. Follow the red arrows to the elevator. The Path has been altered since last you entered. To veer from it is to suffer damnation—"

Stainless steel doors parted smoothly to reveal a corridor of gleaming metal walls and dark plastic floor.

The vampire entered, and began its descent into Hell.

ONE

━━━━━━━━━━━━━━━━━━━━━━━━

SUNSET had caught Oliver Dolan dozing in the Forest of Fernwold. Unless he sped to a haven behind the walls of Fernwold Castle, he feared a nightcreature would catch him as well.

The thought was unpleasant. As Oliver scrambled to his feet and hastily regained the path to the castle, he thrust the idea from his mind. Fear would only make things worse. Panic was to be avoided. He slowed his pace, straightened his lace-cuffed maroon jacket, and smoothed his disheveled auburn locks.

A lad of nineteen summers, Oliver bore the aristocratic features of his family, hereditary rulers of the Dutchy of Fernwold, province of Styx, fourth planet from the G0 star which lent its number to the system. His thin nose tapered to a petite point, emphasizing a sharpness of feature that was softened only by the liquid flow of his wavy hair, the warmth in his brown eyes. His was a face that had seen very little unpleasantness, one that normally wore a smile comfortably, naturally. But at that moment, a distinct frown wrinkled its smoothness.

He'd brought no weapons—not even a dagger.

Traditional weapons of any kind were of dubious utility against the nightcreatures, but certainly something sharp or hard in his hand would have lent more confidence to his gait.

The sun had just dipped below the golden horizon of the forest, dragging precious light behind. It was the moment Oliver had dreaded most of his life. A lover of the trees and fields and waterways of the Duchy, often, on afternoons, he would wander along the paths, through the bowers, over the sparkling, mirror-surfaced streams which burbled happily over smooth-pebbled beds. This day he had paused by a stream for a rest, and had fallen asleep beneath the shady canopy of an oak.

His parents would be worried, he knew, and with good reason.

The light was trickling away rapidly, and darkness filled the sky's inverted bowl with stars. Charon, the larger of Styx's moons, had already risen, shining coolly against the rich blue velvet of the heavens. Puffy gray and white clouds coasted eerily overhead, spurred on by the same steady breeze that whispered through the oaks of the forest disturbing dying leaves which crackled softly, like tiny bones breaking.

The dreamy Nightworld gently seized the land. Soon, its dangers would be unearthed.

Oliver speeded to a jog, then to a slow run which jostled the end of a silk scarf from its nest in his coat. Flaglike, it fluttered behind as he rapidly climbed the path. His calf-high leather boots clopped along the hard-packed earth, kicking loose stones into the mountain laurel that fringed the trail. The darkness began to close around him like a gigantic fist.

From atop a rise in the path, he glimpsed the towers of the castle, proudly thrust above the trees, glowing dully white in the dim beams of Charon and the dusty stars.

No, not far now, he thought. If he could make the road in just a few minutes he would be reasonably safe. The creatures seldom ventured—

A snap. A large branch breaking. The sound was painful to his ears. Startled, he froze, and gazed about him.

He heard the crackle of distant leaves uncaringly stepped upon; then a harsh, brittle *swoosh:* something was moving through the shrubbery.

Three possibilities occurred to the boy: The sounds might have originated from some relatively harmless animal—a squirrel, perhaps, or a bear. But would a squirrel, or even a bear, cause such a din? A man, then. But what would a *man* be doing in the woods at night of his own free will? That left but one possibility, and the realization propelled him into a desperate run down the sloping path, toward the road.

A nightcreature.

Confirming his fears, the noise from the forest behind him rapidly increased. Something was interested in him. Some *thing* was pursuing him.

From behind him came a snarl, then a growl, the staccato rustle of undergrowth violently thrust aside. The thing had increased its speed as well. Shortly it would gain the cleared path, and could apply more speed to the chase.

Oliver whisked off into the night as fast as he could manage. Cold sweat beaded his skin. His face was clammy against the night breeze, but hot and flustered beneath. The trailing end of his scarf snapped. His long hair streamed backward.

He ventured a hurried glance to the rear, where Charon loomed large over the pathway. There was as yet no visible sign of his pursuer. Suddenly his foot struck a large stone embedded in the path, spilling him to the ground. When he raised his dirtied face, he saw it, just gaining the pathway from the dense forest:

A werewolf.

Paralyzed with fear, Oliver could only stare up the hill at the creature silhouetted against the milky white orb of the moon. It halted and raised its flared snout, while inhaling great volumes of fresh air, no doubt full of the scent of Oliver Dolan.

At least seven feet tall, the werewolf seemed all bristling hair, glinting teeth, and unsheathed claws. It stood like a man, on its hind paws, rearing not fifty yards off, a promise of horrible, bloody death.

Momentarily having lost sight of its quarry, the creature growled tentatively, then snapped its fangs with an animal fury made more frightening by its human quality. Oliver, hidden in the shadows, crawled slowly off the path, then rolled into a clump of long grasses. Just as Oliver drove into the deeper shadows, the werewolf began to advance slowly down the incline, slouched forward in predatory expectation. As it neared, Oliver could see that the werewolf wore the tattered clothing of a man, speckled with crusted blood. The creature smelled of earlier meals and offal.

Soon, the beast stood alongside Oliver's hiding place, searching. Its matted brown fur stood on end about its thick neck. Oliver made a conscious effort to restrain his breathing—a very difficult task, considering his run. But he was downwind of the night-creature and it did not seem to have his scent.

Snarling harshly, the werewolf descended the path out of Oliver's view, obviously unwilling to admit that its intended repast was lost. After a few moments, Oliver dared to peek from his hiding place. He craned his neck and found that the werewolf was now out of sight. A few moments' rest to restore his wind, and he crawled warily back toward the pathway. At its edge, his hand brushed a long, stout stick, a poor weapon, but better than nothing.

Grasping this in his right hand, Oliver rose to his knees, and scanned about him. The road could not be more than a hundred yards off. Chances were, the werewolf was still padding along the path, hopeful of espying its quarry once again. Having reached the road, the creature would no doubt retrace its steps.

It would be a disaster if the werewolf caught Oliver

on the pathway. As rapidly as the lad dared, he entered the dark forest that separated him from the relative safety of the road. After penetrating some way into the foliage, he could advance once more toward the road. From there he had a fighting chance to sprint for the safety of the nearby castle.

He moved cautiously. After a minute or two of steady, if somewhat noisy progress through clumps of blackberry bushes and tangles of fallen tree limbs, he angled toward the road. Crisp dead leaves carpeted the dank, musky forest floor and crunched under Oliver's stealthy footsteps. Bent conifers surrounded him now, like gnarled soldiers standing a long forgotten post.

As he walked, the boy yearned for the security to be found behind the stout walls of the castle. There he could pull a chair up to a warm muttering fire, switch on a lamp, and read while munching an apple. Dwelling on this image helped to keep him calm.

Suddenly a thick-boled tree loomed before him, its dense canopy blocking the little light that remained. Here, the moon's pale beams barely reached the ground, sufficient only to mottle the darkness.

And so Oliver did not see his nemesis until the moment it hurled itself upon him from behind the tree.

Snarling, drool slathering its chin, the beast jumped with such force that it impaled itself on the sharp end of Oliver's branch. It was not driven far enough into the beast's abdomen to destroy the creature, for the force wrenched it from Oliver's grip.

The hulking werewolf raised its head to the sky and screamed in pain. Glistening blood streamed from its wound as it staggered about, clawing at the stick.

Recovering from his shock rapidly, Oliver dashed toward the road. The creature quickly plucked the stake from its body, swiveled about, and fiercely followed its intended victim.

Oliver ran breathlessly, unmindful of the prickly holly and the blackberry thorns that tore at his clothes, raked his face. Somehow his feet avoided the snares set by weeds and branches. Very quickly, he found the road.

As he paused briefly to suck in some air, he heard the squeaking of carriage wheels and the clop of horses' hooves. He glanced down the dirt road to where the castle could clearly be seen. Rolling slowly toward the huge walls, rocking noisily on overworked springs, was a gray, wooden van pulled by two brown and white horses.

If he could but attract the driver's attention . . .

"Help!" he cried, with what little power remained to his lungs. "Stop!"

His limbs heavy with pain, he staggered forward. Behind him, the frenzied thrashing made by the werewolf drew nearer. The sound triggered a burst of speed into his legs.

Then the forest sounds ceased; the werewolf was on the road as well. Even as the young man reached this conclusion, the beast's grunts and snarls snapped at his ears.

The van *had* stopped, he suddenly realized, and he added a final burst of speed. A hairy face peered inquisitively around its side. Not daring to halt, Oliver scrambled up to the driver's seat. He flailed wildly at the man and yelled, "Drive, man! Start moving!"

"Whoa, lad. Steady on. I'll deal with the matter. Up to the roof with you." There was no need for further encouragement; Oliver leaped to the flat roof. "You'll be safer there."

Oliver looked back. The werewolf was almost upon them. "Hurry!" he cried down to the man. "Whip your team, man. Let's get out of here!"

"Oh, there's no hope of escaping the thing," the stranger said, unruffled. "We'll just have to meet it here. Now, why don't you stand up, so the beast can see you plainly. That will distract it long enough for me to do what I must."

Startled, Oliver stared down at the fellow in disbelief. The stranger was crawling into the van through a door behind the driver's seat. It was well that Oliver was crouched, for suddenly the van was struck with such force that he was tossed backward. The lad clung to the stout wooden luggage mounts to save himself from tumbling over the side.

He turned.

The werewolf was trying to clamber atop with him. Inch-long claws scrabbled at the wooden surface Oliver lay upon, leaving deep white scars. Suddenly, he was staring the thing in the eyes.

The face was an obscene meld of man and beast. Baleful fires flickered in large eyes, and malodorous saliva dripped from sharp, ivory-bright fangs that opened and then gnashed together in noisy anticipation of a hard-won meal.

Oliver pulled off his soft coat and hurled it. The jacket wrapped itself neatly around the thing's head; without daring to consider the consequences, Oliver stood and booted the werewolf squarely in the snout.

The creature whimpered with pain, then howled, but did not budge. Holding itself fast with one paw, it swiped at Oliver and knocked the boy to the road. He landed well, but the fall dazed him; he could barely move. His breath seemed squeezed from his lungs. Helpless, he watched the werewolf rip the coat from its face then glare about, searching. Finally, its eyes settled on Oliver and snarling a savage victory note through its teeth, it hopped down.

Though energy quickly returned to his numbed limbs, Oliver could nevertheless only crawl backwards, crab-like.

"Now then," called a voice from behind. "I think we've found what's needed for this little dilemma."

The fat man now stood alongside the van, a top hat of fine beaver perched slightly askew atop a great cherubic head, black suede cape bellying in the breeze. Strapped to his paunch was a large metal cylinder. Both hands gripped a two-pronged spear attached to the canister by a long, thin wire.

The stranger's beefy features were set in a grim smile. No fear showed.

"All right, lad. Just move slowly away from the field of honor. Easy now. I've got its attention. We don't want it back at you."

Oliver crept cautiously away from the van toward the roadside. The werewolf seemed to have lost interest in him, staring instead with great intensity at the obese newcomer, as though, somehow, it knew him.

Tentatively at first, then roaring a challenge that caused a tingle to race through Oliver, it moved a step forward. The fat man took a corresponding step toward the creature, waggling the spear teasingly.

The werewolf charged.

Raising his spear and dropping to one knee, the man caught the beast full in its hirsute chest with the barbed prongs. Hardly fazed, the furious nightcreature slashed at the man with its claws, trying all the while to press forward. But it was halted by the spear, and the spear only.

Oliver saw no hope for the man, or for himself. After all, it took more to kill a werewolf than a bident and bravery. What could the fellow have been thinking?

Calmly, the fat man inserted the unoccupied end of the weapon into a slot on the canister. His agile right hand quickly flipped a switch on the device.

There was a buzzing hum. Abruptly, the werewolf ceased snarling, then stiffened and tried to back away, to pull itself from the prongs. But the barbs prevented that. The caped man followed, hit another switch.

The werewolf howled like a damned soul and jerked about as if in the throes of some strange affliction. Wisps of gray smoke began to rise from its chest and face and a tongue of flame licked at the dark through a tapered ear. Oliver heard a crackle, smelled the stench of burnt flesh—and something else.

"There!" the fat man said, satisfied. "One more power surge." Another switch clicked. Completely out of control, the werewolf weaved to and fro, clutching at the spear frantically, shrieking with pain and outrage.

The animal dropped to the road. Quivering, it began to burn.

The caped man wrinkled his nose at the stench, then pushed at a lever near the base of the spear. The weapon's barbs retracted; he pulled it free easily, then let his mechanism slip to the ground. He hopped blithely over to his van, returned with a smaller canister, and squirted the flames with white, bubbly foam. They died.

After returning his weapon to the van, the stranger poked at the dead hulk with a stick. "Big fellow," he muttered. Then, remembering Oliver, he turned to face him. "Come here, lad. You might as well have a look at the beastie who almost had you."

Oliver obeyed.

"Here. You'll need some light." The man pulled an electric torch from a large pocket and flashed it over the corpse. "I'll bet you think this is all supernatural."

"Magical, sir!" Oliver breathed, "and you, sir, must be a magician, or a sorcerer, even."

The man swept up a hand gracefully in what seemed a practiced mannerism. "Tut tut. Nothing of the sort. Possessed of a little more knowledge than your people, and certainly owner of more advanced equipment, but a sorcerer? Hardly. Although I *can* see how all this might appear supernatural." He offered a manicured hand. "By the way, the name's Geoffrey. Geoffrey Turner, member of the Holy Order to Preserve the Empire. And what name do you go by, lad?"

Oliver hesitantly grasped the man's hand, pumped it. "Oliver Dolan, sir." He waved his free hand toward the castle. "My family rules this land. By day, anyway."

"My word, how fortunate," the man said, rubbing his long, bushy beard in contemplation. "It would appear that I'll have little trouble finding shelter for this night. But first, I want you to have a closer look at our dead friend here."

He cast the torch-beam down, overturned the ruined creature with his stick.

Oliver gasped. Instead of burned flesh and singed

fur, he noted the gleam of metal, lengths of discolored wiring, items of half-melted plastic and hard glass he had never encountered before.

"An android, Oliver," explained Turner. "Part flesh, part robot. They're all this way—the werewolves, the dragons, the gryphons, the chimeras, and what have you." He plucked a white silk handkerchief trimmed with blue lace from a pocket of his beige, ruffled shirt and dabbed at his damp forehead. "Yes, and even the vampires, the most dangerous of the lot."

The vampire's boots clicked against the jet floor of the hallway, echoing loudly in the normally soundless corridor.

Along the right wall, red arrows blinked brightly, darting crimson flashes into the dimly lit hall, directing the creature to an open elevator.

The vampire entered and doors whisked shut behind it.

The mechanism sighed deep into the heart of the Netherworld.

Had the vampire known of Christian legend, of Dante's Inferno, it might have found the situation ironic. To descend to Hell in an elevator—Evil as a machine—a fantastic notion, worthy of a painting by Bosch.

But this vampire knew little save of its Nightworld, of its Master's will, of its hunger. Even now, its insides ached at the thought of fresh, warm blood. But the audience would not be long. And then it could stalk its prey.

Suddenly, the elevator halted. The doors opened.

The scent of molten brimstone caused its nostrils to flare. Moaning, weeping, and the gnashing of teeth assailed its ears.

The hot breath of Hell caressed its face.

TWO

‹›‹›‹›‹›‹›‹›‹›‹›‹›‹›‹›‹›‹›‹›‹›

WHEN he descended from his bath that evening wearing crisp white slacks, a lavender quilt lounge jacket and a rose cravat, Oliver found his father Dudley, Viscount Dolan, hoisting mead with his new friend Geoffrey Turner. They sat at a long, rough-planed oak table, under an ancient chandelier which sported tiny electric light bulbs. In the nearby hearth, a sputtering fire hissed smoky warmth into the cavernous hall. The odor of fresh-cooked venison lingered in the air.

Over the uplifted silver rim of his cup, Turner noted Oliver's return. "Ah, here's the lad." The man's plump red face, flushed further with pleasure as he waved his free hand, gestured Oliver toward a seat.

Settled in the high-backed chair, Oliver glanced hesitantly at his father, a gaunt man who seldom smiled. At that moment his features, a somber collection of angles and etched shadows only faintly softened by the wrinkles of age, were bent into an unusually deep frown. Oliver found his father's serious gaze upon him and could not help but avert his eyes.

"As I mentioned earlier, Mr. Turner," the elder Dolan said in a quiet but resonant voice, "Oliver's mother and I do not know how properly to express our thanks for your rescue of our son. We can but offer hospitality and shelter for as long as you should require it, anytime." He lifted his pewter cup with a thin, blue-veined hand, drained it.

"Think nothing of it," the fat man replied. He stifled a belch. "My job, dealing with creatures like that, don't you know. Dispatched a hundred werewolves if I've dispatched a one."

"Oliver," Lord Dolan said in a soft but urgent voice. "I trust that an exercise of such poor precaution on your part will not recur."

"There, there, your lordship," Turner interrupted. "The lad handled himself quite well, I think. No need to be overly stern. One cannot go long in this world without eventually encountering the Nightworld crew."

"Nevertheless," Oliver's mother interjected as she refilled the goblets. The white lace on her cuff and about her neck shook with her movement. She wore a pink and beige evening dress reserved for guests—Oliver's favorite, bustle, pleated frills and all. "Oliver should have been more cautious. Asleep in the forest at dusk! He might as well have taken a dive off the topmost of our towers!" Even in middle age, Lady Dolan was a beautiful woman. Tall, slender, graceful, she provided the proper contrast to her darker, dour husband. Her long, lazily curling cream-blonde hair was a casual frame to the even proportions of her face. Behind her mild appearance, though, lay an essential sternness, a strong, stubborn will that made her pale blue eyes her dominant feature, as she turned them, scolding, to her son. "But I suppose the episode is now properly a thing of the past and best forgotten. Another cup of mead, Mr. Turner?"

"Don't mind if I do," he said, flashing a ready smile at the attractive woman through his dark beard.

Lady Jessica refilled her husband's cup as well, and allowed Oliver a half portion. Its honey and alcohol breath was sweet under Oliver's nose. "Now, if you gentlemen will excuse me, I must retire. Worrying about Oliver this evening has been quite exhausting." She exited regally, leaving behind the subtle scent of jasmine.

Absently, the Viscount waved good-bye, then returned to his guest. "You were saying, Mr. Turner? I must confess, communication between our provinces is uncommon. I have heard of your group, vaguely and not always in good terms—but, I am most intrigued as to its origins, and purpose."

Pausing first to sip at his mead, Turner sprawled back in his chair, arranging his loose pilot coat into a more comfortable hanging on his hefty frame. His face assumed a serious aspect. "First, Lord Viscount Dolan, you dwell in a particularly isolated section of the world." He gestured around him. "I see that you retain some of the electrical conveniences. Lighting. A few appliances. Yet your culture is principally agrarian, I think."

"We do maintain relations with two other communities. As to the so-called conveniences, they have existed for as long as we have records. Power is supplied by a generator harnessed to a nearby waterfall."

"Not far from the norm on Styx—an almost medieval life-style, robed in the garb of Standard Victorian."

"I don't understand," the Viscount said, a hint of displeasure in his tone.

"Ah, yes, the way Styx used to be, under the Empire and its Queen . . ." Turner's eyes grew far away. They were brown eyes, soft eyes, the most expressive parts of an eloquent face. He blinked. "Oh, forgive me. I do go on sometimes. But it does trouble me how far Styx has descended from its former ideal state. Ah—I've lost you. Never mind. Perhaps you've heard tell of this before. Perhaps you know only sections of it through whatever legends you have hereabouts."

He cleared his throat. His voice was a tenor that occasionally ranged to baritone for emphasis.

"Sir, as you well know, this is a benighted world. But

such has not always been the case. At one time, it was part of a great Empire that spanned many stars."

"Surely all that is only myth," Lord Dolan protested abruptly, hand impatiently toying with a lock of his thinning hair.

"Please, sir, I assure you that all I say is fact. All the circumstances fit. It alone could be the truth concerning conditions here on Styx. You saw the carcass of the werewolf, did you not?"

"Indeed," Viscount Dolan admitted sullenly. "Its insides were filled with the stuff of magic." Taking a snuff box from his mauve waistcoat pocket, he sniffed some of the strong-smelling stuff as Turner continued.

"No. There, sir, you are wrong. Those things you saw were of *technology,* a result of *science.* There is nothing supernatural about them. The creature was created, yes. But not by immaterial dark forces. Please, allow me to explain.

"Centuries ago, this world was a colony of an empire in space. For reasons of its own, that Empire designed this world in a style which belonged to a time centuries past on the Homeworld. But then, the Empire suddenly died, or, at any rate, lost contact with this world.

"Styx's technological facilities, which were quite extensive, were regulated by a machine—an incredibly complex machine called a *Computer,* situated somewhere deep below the surface of the planet. For some reason, the Computer malfunctioned, doing strange things to the environment, manufacturing hideous creatures, and recreating terrible mythological conditions modeled on the many legends of Homeworld's myth-rich past."

"Nonsense," the Viscount said quietly. He blew his nose into a fine linen handkerchief. "Virtual and utter nonsense."

"Please, sir. If I may finish," Turner said, only slightly vexed by the man's obstinacy. "After the fall of the Empire, and the malfunction of the planetwide communications network, extraordinary things began to happen. The provinces began to forget the truth of their origins. They withdrew into their separate existences—just as you of Fernwold Castle maintain almost total independence. They came to regard the scientific facts of their existence as mere myth. They regressed to the social situations which were meant to serve only as their models. Fortunately, among the record-keepers of these communities, some fought this inexplicable loss of memory. They realized it was the work of some malevolent force, and they banded together . . . their original number now is gone but their descendants continue the work, seeking to rid the land of the nightmarish beasts that stalk by night, and seeking a way to kill the evil in this world at its roots."

There was an uncomfortable lull in the conversation.

"And yet you know nothing of the real cause. A few suspicions, nothing more," the Viscount said finally, rapping a genteel fist on the table. "Can you not acknowledge that the force of evil is indeed supernatural, that war is being waged here on Styx between *spiritual* forces, those of good, and those of evil—not by some machine?"

"I have nothing solid with which to prove to you now that such is not the case. I do know that if spiritual forces are warring as you claim, the evil faction at least may be dealt with in quite physical terms. Its representatives are mere constructs—flesh-clothed machines. Powerful, true, yet vulnerable to certain methods. The werewolf, for example, Oliver. You must know something of electricity, since you live in a castle with electric lights. The device strapped to me was simply a powerful battery. Each of the prongs of the spear was an electrode. Merely by sticking the werewolf in the right spot, I shorted its electronic circuitry. Now, would you call that a *supernatural* process?"

"I must admit," said Oliver in a low voice, "it seemed so at the time." He shifted uncomfortably. The air seemed much too warm where he sat by the blazing logs.

"Ah yes, I suppose it would. To less advanced cultures, advanced technology might as well *be* magic."

"Would you tell us your suspicions concerning the power behind these creatures?" the Viscount requested politely.

"Gladly. I was about to, as a matter of fact." Turner cleared his throat gruffly. "It is our fraternity's belief that the World Computer which was originally responsible for the way things are, could not have done it alone. No. There was, and *is* a human being behind the situation. As to whether he is still alive, we do not know. But a thinking, reasoning force lies behind all this, albeit *quite* mad. We believe that if the Computer can be destroyed, this world can return to normalcy. Perhaps equipment can be found to communicate with what remains of the Empire. But most important is the halting of the reign of terror that has existed on Styx these past centuries.

"Now, to the reason I've come this way. It is said that somewhere to the west a spacecraft has landed."

"A *what?*" The Viscount's eyebrows rose in perplexity.

"A spaceship. A vessel from another world. Perhaps an emissary from the remains of the original Empire, come to communicate again with this faraway colony. We must contact the spacecraft, not only to reestablish communication with the other worlds in the galaxy, but to obtain the knowledge and the equipment needed to defeat the creature who holds Styx in thrall and plays with it so malevolently." Here, he paused and sighed. "Unfortunately, we do not know the exact place of descent of the ship. Our small number have divided, and are presently searching. Along the way we are, of course, only too happy to dispose of whatever beasts and nightcreatures we encounter. But what I need from you, now, is information. Have you heard anything of such a craft in the nearby land, or of a great light falling from the heavens?"

"Nothing, I fear."

"Ah, well. I suppose I'll have to journey farther west

before I hear tidings of the thing." He looked at Oliver. "And you? Have you heard aught of what I speak?"

Oliver shook his head.

"Well, so much for that," Turner grumbled. "I just hope we can find this spaceship before *he* does."

"*He*, Mr. Turner? Just a moment ago, you were referring to *it*."

Turner chuckled ruefully. "After our talk of spiritual forces, you'll enjoy this, Viscount." His chuckle turned into a belly-laugh. "The Computer, or creature if you will, has a name for itself."

"Indeed?"

"Yes." Turner ceased laughing and became darkly reflective. "It calls itself Satan."

"Enter, my Servant," boomed a sonorous voice from the darkness.

The vampire obeyed without hesitation, stepping into the wide room. From all around came the menacing hiss of fire. Along the path, flames leapt into the blackness, illuminating at random, simulated rock-walled chambers, each inhabited by human forms in poses of agony and degradation. With its acute hearing, the creature noted that the wretched cries were but recordings.

"To the rear of the hall, my vampire," said the voice.

The vampire followed it, moving around columns resembling stalagmites and stalactites.

"Hold."

The vampire halted.

"Behold your Master."

Bright illumination shot up in the corner, flowing along a large section of wall. Gnarled, twisted machinery abounded. Mirror-bright puddles lay where molten metal once had flowed. Like dead vines, cables hung in disarray from the cinder-spattered ceiling.

Long consoles, and banks of tape transports stretched interminably into the darkness, humming, clicking, working.

Suspended in the glassy heart of one machine, immersed in a nutrient bath, and festooned with wires connecting him to the Computer, was the Master.

"Bow to the Prince of Darkness," the deep, dreadful voice demanded. The Master's lips did not move.

21

They were hardly lips at all, mere flaps of white skin barely covering the teeth, set in a permanent deathly leer.

The vampire obediently whisked its cape around and executed a deep bow.

"Rise."

The vampire rose.

"I have summoned you because there is danger afoot. Danger to us. Danger that must be dealt with."

No emotion crossed the travesty of a face in the bath. The eyes had long ago bulged into a fixed stare. Exposed veins pulsed in one temple. Wisps of white hair lay slack against the pale pate.

"A remnant of the forces of God has fallen from the sky. Those that oppose us here on Styx would find it, establish contact with the Others from Beyond, find weapons that would do us harm."

There was an ominous stillness. The thing that had once been human shuddered slightly, rippling the surface of its bath.

"We must find the fallen spacecraft before the Enemies. We must destroy it, and its inhabitants. I will channel all my powers into this task and I have special duties for you. Do you feel yourself capable?"

Bowing slightly, the vampire nodded. "Yes, Satan."

"Excellent. There is a certain man. He has been my particular bane for some time. We have received a brief transmission from the photosensors of a werewolf terminated this evening. We know where he is and where he is headed. You will journey immediately to Haven 911. If the man gets that far, you shall waylay him."

"Who is this man, Master?"

"He goes by the name of Geoffrey Turner."

"Ah." *The vampire nodded.* "Turner."

THREE

Alone, he stood in a bog.

Nightmists had stealthily surrounded him, a legion of wraiths dancing slowly around the melancholy cypresses surrounding the quagmire. Above, the two crescent moons were aligned as though some watcher in the skies stared down malevolently. Not a yard from him, a fetid pool began to bubble. Fascinated, he stared down as a clawed hand broke the surface, then snaked forward and grasped his ankle.

He tried to scream but could not. Distant laughter mocked him.

Suddenly the muck boiled furiously and another matted paw reached up to snag the solid ground upon which he stood. A head emerged, unmistakable: a werewolf. Slowly the creature rose from the pool, dragging itself onto firm land. Its wet fur stank of ooze. Its faceplate was shorn off, revealing mechanical and electronic parts drenched with gore.

The werewolf released his leg, stood, stared at Oliver with eyes that were not bestial, but quite human. "We wait for you in Hell," it rasped, blood dripping from its canines. "We wait for your soul."

The beast suddenly raked out at him with its claws.

Oliver woke, sweating. Twisted bedclothes lay about him. He was in his bed, then. A nightmare. Only a nightmare.

He sighed. Rising, he made for the window, opened it and drew fresh, cold, pine-scented air into his lungs. A breeze gently fingered Oliver's gray woolen sleeping gown and pinched the bare flesh beneath with its chill. Gazing out above the battlements of the castle, over the silent pines and oaks of the forest to the frosted peaks of the Mountains of Stillness, he pondered the nightmares his land held.

He wondered if the strange man who had saved him was right. All his brief life he had been trained to believe that in God lay the sole hope of salvation from the forces of Evil; that by believing in Him, trusting solely in His mercy, one's soul might rise to Heaven after its test in the crucible of this existence.

And now this fat man had come, bringing with him a peculiar secular salvation from the clutches of the werewolf. Turner had sown the seeds of doubt in Oliver's fertile imagination.

The young man's thoughts turned to the implications of Turner's words. Oliver had known only one philosophy in his life. He could not contend with all of the possibilities suddenly presented with the advent of Geoffrey Turner.

Driving such thoughts from his head, the lad bowed and muttered a short prayer of supplication. He would seek counsel with Reverend Marshall later that day, he decided. When he raised his head, dawn had paled the sky and brought a blush to the horizon. Soon the sun would peek up over the rim of the world, chase the Nightrealm away for another day.

As he watched, the light flowed slowly about the massive castle walls, casting friendly shadows across the cobbled roads of the small town behind it. Lights flickered on in thatch-roofed cottages as the farmers

made ready to continue their harvest of the wheat
fields outside the walls.

It was a heartening sight. Much relieved, Oliver
returned to bed and slept peacefully.

As heir apparent to his father's titles and duties,
Oliver's principal occupation during his youth had
been the acquisition of the education necessary to
shoulder such responsibilities. Of late, he had even
assumed some of the Viscount's burden; he was
working.

At a reasonable hour of the morning, after a sleep
untroubled by further nightmares, Oliver rose, breakfasted, and set about his tasks.

Harvest time had arrived: the wheat, corn, oats,
barley, and other essential foodstuffs that had been
sown in early spring had matured. Now they were
being reaped, milled, and stored.

A traditional duty of the ruler of Fernwold Duchy
was to oversee the harvest, to ensure that everything
went properly. Dudley Dolan had, that year, assigned
the northwest quadrant to Oliver, and, as the lad had
taken interest in the grain harvest since he was old
enough to walk beyond the castle walls, he had no
difficulty supervising the harvest. Indeed, often he'd
worn old clothes in the fields, driven the reapers, or
helped to gather the grain, had tossed the crop harvest
onto carts, and helped drive it to the silos.

The folk of Fernwold, for this and more, thought
much of him. There were no strict stratifications of
society in the walled town, but it was seldom that a
person, of any rank, in command, would dirty his
hands with the common lot of workers. It was generally agreed that Oliver would make a fine Viscount.

The harvest had gone well. The fields were almost
bare. Another day or two of gleaning, some compost,
a little manure, and the land would be ready to winter.
Come spring, the eternal cycle would begin once more.
To celebrate the bountiful offering of the land, Lord
Dolan had declared that Field Feasts were to be held

late that afternoon, the principal celebration to take place in the grassy gaming courts adjacent to the southern battlements. It was to be a simple enough gathering. People would bring their own food to be placed on long oaken tables for the enjoyment of all. Dance, gaming, and song would provide the entertainment—and the festivities would conclude with a short ceremony of thanksgiving led by a minister or two. Then the people would clean up after themselves, and be off to their various domiciles in Fernwold Town.

The morning's work went well. Oliver, pleased with the efforts of the townspeople, dismissed them before the noon meal to allow time to prepare for the Field Feast. This was not entirely for unselfish reasons, for he very much wished to speak to the man who had saved his life the previous evening.

Strolling purposefully along the hall adjacent to the bedrooms of the castle, after discarding his gritty workclothes and donning comfortable black lamb's wool breeches and a soft cotton shirt, Oliver heard a sound from the chamber provided for Geoffrey Turner's use. Though he'd been heading to the dining hall for lunch, thoughts of the delicious food troubling his stomach, he stopped a moment and listened.

The sound again . . . a groan!

Concerned, Oliver eased the heavy oaken door open, quietly peered into the still darkness of the curtained room. Perhaps the brave fellow had sustained an injury he was too proud to admit.

The room smelled of sleep and stale liquor. Another groan was heard, deeper, longer, from the bed. He also heard another, stranger, fainter sound—a slight *hum* or a *whir*. A strange sort of snore, thought Oliver. "Mr. Turner," he whispered, vexed—wanting to speak to the man, yet not wanting to trouble him. "Sir, are you all right?"

The young man tiptoed across the room, careful not to scuff the wood floor with his leather boots. It was far too dark to see, so he moved to the window and flung open the drapes. A shaft of light immediately angled onto the face of the man swathed in sheets and blankets.

"Arrgh!" Turner cried. "Close those bleeding things! Oooh, my head!" He threw a blanket over his face, burrowed his substantial form deeper into the soft feather bed. The springs creaked beneath his weight.

"Pardon me, Mr. Turner," Oliver said, sliding the curtain almost closed. "I was passing, and I thought I heard you groan. Are you all right?"

"Yes," Turner said, his voice muffled by the bedclothes. "Just a bit worse for wear—last night's ordeal, you know."

Oliver felt a pang of guilt. "Sir, I feel somewhat responsible. Shall I fetch a physician? Are you wounded?" He moved anxiously to the bedside. All he could see of Turner was a tuft of disheveled hair.

"What?" A bloodshot eye peeked out. "Oh, dear boy, not *that* ordeal. Goodness knows, that was but a trifle. I mean the incredibly potent mead with which your father waylays unsuspecting passersby. A bottle of that stuff's enough to eat a man's liver and I had two bottles' worth, at least. Ouch! Hurts to think."

Relieved, yet still concerned, Oliver remarked that a doctor might still be in order. The suggestion had a remarkable effect upon the man. Turner immediately sat up. "Oh, no. No. That's not necessary, lad. Uhm— don't bother yourself—I'll live." He slowly peeled off the sheets and blankets and lay in the whiteness, looking like a beached whale. "A glass of water. That's what I need. And a brief visit to my van, where I've a few necessary—uhm, *medicinal* tools— of healing, you know. And then something to eat. That'll fix me up just fine. Must face it. Can't stay here groaning all day. What time *is* it?"

Oliver checked his wristwatch. It was an ancient one. The devices were rare now, and repairing their spring-driven motors was an art. His mother had given one to him on his eighteenth birthday. "A little after one o'clock."

"Lord!" responded the fat man, heaving himself out of bed. "If you'll fetch me that water, I'll be dressed by the time you return."

Oliver nodded and departed the man, who was groaning and sighing as he slipped on his clothing.

"So then," said an obviously well Geoffrey Turner, after washing his last piece of steamy venison pie down with a swallow of foamy lager. "You, promised me a turn about the premises."

"In return for a look into your van," Oliver reminded him as he grabbed a gleaming red apple from the mound of fruit centering the table.

"And I must see about organizing some of the entertainment for the Field Feasts," said Lady Jessica, delicately dabbing at her mouth with a cloth napkin. "I trust you will enjoy our little celebration, Mr. Turner," she added graciously. She frowned slightly as the fat man helped himself to yet another pull from the beer keg. Although she took an occasional glass of sherry, she was famed for disapproval of regular drinking.

Oliver considered his mother. She was a handsome woman. In her time, she'd been quite a beauty. She was not of Fernwold, but rather from Salisbury, a duchy farther west, with which Fernwold regularly traded. The population centers of Styx tended to be a day's ride apart so as to render night travel unnecessary. Viscount Dolan had been visiting Salisbury on matters of commerce, when he met Jessica Fielding. Though Oliver occasionally heard rumors that their romance had been stormy, his father and mother now seemed quite settled.

Oliver had mixed feelings about his mother. He loved her deeply, yet resented her possessiveness. He was her only child, and he felt it was almost as if she wished him to remain a child all his life. Although she tolerated his casual interest in the young girls of Fernwold, she was obviously not thrilled at their apparent interest in him.

"Yes, my lady," answered Turner, giving her a friendly-bear smile that only fat men seem capable of mustering successfully. "I feel quite fortunate, privileged even, to have arrived at this opportune time."

"How long exactly do you plan to stay?" she asked, more calculation than warmth in her voice.

Turner's left eyebrow rose a trifle. "Ah—I thought tomorrow morning would be a good time to depart. Must be about my mission."

"Oh? So soon, Mr. Turner?" she said.

"I fear so."

"Well, Oliver," she commanded, rising from the table, resplendent in her day dress. "See that Mr. Turner enjoys every instant of his brief stay with us." She nodded politely, turned, and swept away with a rustle of her red satin and corded silk skirts.

"Ah, lad," Turner said, again filling his goblet with beer, "I fear your mother doesn't approve of the likes of me. A stranger, deep in the depravity of drink, come to demoralize her only son."

"If it weren't for you, sir, I wouldn't be around to demoralize. I'm sure she realizes that."

"Enough of this 'sir' and 'Mr. Turner' business, young fellow!" Turner rose imperiously from the table, settling his black beaver on his curls. "In the future you may call me simply 'Geoffrey'. Right? Right. So, let's be about our tour."

First, Oliver led Turner through the interior of the castle's keep. Here the director of the community's army of defense—the castellan—resided. The army itself consisted of able-bodied men of Fernwold able to contribute spare hours to drilling and to patrolling the battlements of the encircling walls. The settlement was fortunately situated atop a steep slope, rendering at least half of the wall practically impervious to attack. The other sections of curtain and towers were more strongly reinforced, studded with arrow slits, and gun placements. Cannon could not be used; the recoil would shatter the walls or tower. The defense measures, as stringent as they were, would not have held up against an attacking army of similar ingenuity and armament. However, the nightcreatures tended to roam the night alone. Only occasionally had they been known to lay siege to a castle, and even then, restricted to night, their attempts generally failed. Tunnels burrowed under the walls to collapse them could be easily filled in by day. Stones worked out of the thick wall could be fixed and mortared back in place. Nevertheless, oral and written history was stocked with fearful tales of provinces overrun by Satan's minions, their inhabitants subjected to awful fates.

Oliver led Turner to a cupola which overlooked the entirety of Fernwold Town, the forty-foot walls of the community, and the surrounding fields, forests, and streams. The Town was a neat grouping of some three hundred white-washed stuccoed buildings, most with quaint thatched roofs.

"Quite like many of the provincial communities I've visited," Turner commented briefly, the breeze tugging lazily at his longish, curling hair. "Very comfortable, very snug."

"The people are happy enough, I suppose," said Oliver.

"Are they? Growth limited by strict population control; antiquated machinery falling apart daily; the constant threat of very real and physical danger; evenings spiced with supernatural dread; monsters roaming the verges by night? Do you really think they're happy when they must constantly fear that their community will be overrun by the forces of the Devil himself?" He made a sweeping gesture toward the walls, the town, the neat grassy fields where cattle grazed, the fall-painted forests ribboned by sparkling rivers and creeks. "All this, my lad, all this was once a paradise. And you can see the beauty of it even now. But what you *can't* see, my boy, what you can't make out down there, are the hidden beasts who patrol the nights of this world, the creatures who would make us all slaves of Satan." He drew in a deep, clean breath. "And the mindless *fear,* the *dread* of the supernatural in the hearts of your people." He pointed at Oliver. "In *your* heart!"

Oliver shuddered. He looked away.

"Ignorance," Turner continued, his voice mounting in anger, "ignorance and stupid, irrational *religion*—that's what's preventing Styx from becoming the world of greatness it was destined to be. If we can *unite* the provinces, perhaps we'll have a chance to battle the evil that holds this planet in thrall."

The words "religion" and "evil" caused Oliver to remember that he had promised himself to visit a minister. He felt obligated to defend his religion's views on Styx. "If we believe in God, Geoffrey, if we trust in Him, surely He will save us."

"Did God save you last night?"

"He brought you to me."

"Pah! If God is so concerned about his people, why doesn't he strike Satan down? Why must we all suffer in this beautiful, terrible, frustrating *Hell?*"

"But Styx is a testing ground," Oliver objected. "We won't survive in this existence. Whether we're destroyed by a Satanic creature or we die of old age, what's important is that our *faith* survives. For *faith* is the weapon that will defeat the legions of Hell."

Turner harrumphed mightily. "Did faith kill that werewolf last night? No. Science did. *Technology.* The product of knowledge, Oliver." He stabbed a forefinger westward. "Out there is the fallen ship, a product of the science that *made* this world, fellow. And in that spacecraft is our hope of ridding ourselves of the evil in this world, destroying the ignorance that darkens Styx just as much as Nightworld does. Here—you wanted to see the inside of my van. Well, let me tell you, much of its content was built ages ago. But I had enough knowledge to modify those old instruments into weapons and to use them effectively. They are products of a greater civilization, a peak in life that we can achieve again! Let's go down. I'll show them to you. Maybe you'll think twice about this religious claptrap you've been mouthing so glibly."

He pivoted, then huffed and puffed excitedly down the winding stairway, trailing his cape and his indignation. Oliver had to hurry to catch up with the agitated man. Should he look inside the van? Perhaps he'd better have a talk with an elder, first, to prepare his spirit for what he might find there.

His curiosity got the better of his guilt. He followed the waddling man all the way to the stable where Turner's horses placidly munched Fernwold oats. Nearby his van was parked before a vacant stall. Grumbling, Turner flung open the back door, reached inside, and flipped a switch. The interior lit up. "There. How's that for starters?"

Oliver glanced around for a connection to the castle's power supply, but could see no electrical cord. Puzzled, he gazed up at the man.

"A very powerful battery," explained Turner. "Much bigger than the one I used to destroy that nightcreature last evening. Ever see anything like it?"

"No," conceded Oliver. He had not.

"That's just the beginning. Hop on in. Have a look." After pulling himself up through the doorway, Turner held out a beefy hand to assist Oliver's entrance. Inside, Oliver's eyes opened wide with surprise. The interior was walled in metal. "I occasionally have to make a night of it here. Tempered steel, Oliver." He struck the shiny stuff with a knuckle. "Haven't found a nightcreature yet that can get through that!" Turner gestured toward the front of the van. "Scoot up there, lad. I want to show you something."

They skirted the rumpled cot and passed a panel filled with odd instruments and closed cabinets. Into the van Oliver noted a stronger version of the odor that clung about Geoffrey Turner's person: a combination of cologne, alcohol, pipe tobacco and something indefinable. The atmosphere of the enclosure was one of shabby gentility. Directing Oliver to sit in a chair firmly welded to the metal floor, Turner pressed a button. There was a whir, a click. As Oliver sat in the cushioned seat, a black shutter buzzed open in front of him giving a broad view, through thick glass, of what lay before the van. "What's this for?" he asked, patting the spoked wheel before him.

"You'll note that there are numerous pedals and buttons placed about you. Controls. The wheel is one of the controls."

"Controls? For what?"

"If need be, this van can drive itself. Its battery is linked to a complicated drive unit. Should I lose my horses or find it necessary to have more speed, I simply drive the van by its own power. I don't like to do this— rather, I do it as seldom as possible. It makes people think I'm some sort of magician, and among primitives advanced science is usually mistaken for a manifestation of evil. But when I must travel some distance between duchies, when I know I'll have to travel by night or stop for rest at night, I abandon my horses—sell them at some community, you know—and strike out on my own. Quite a bit of power in one of these batteries. Which reminds me . . ." He tapped a dial-face with a fingernail. "I really should hook an extension to Fernwold's power supply. Not that I'm terribly low— I just don't like to chance not being able to get more elsewhere for a while. Think your sire will mind? Oliver, are you listening to me?"

But Oliver was quite lost in his thoughts on the implications of a horseless carriage. "You mean you just get inside, and drive this thing—without horses?"

"That's what I said, didn't I?"

"Yes, of course, but . . ."

Turner clapped a hand on the youth's shoulder. "A bit astonishing, what? You'll see *more* astonishing things, let me tell you. They're all applications of science and technology, Oliver. Faith doesn't run this thing. Religion doesn't supply the power. It's a combination of mechanics and electricity—pure and simple. Much simpler than the level of technological sophistication obviously owned by Satan. But here, let me show you more." The fat man tugged Oliver, reluctant to leave the driver's chair, back toward the rear. "Here is the device I used to short circuit the werewolf-android," said Turner, tapping the weapon, racked on a wall. He showed Oliver larger versions for dealing with larger monsters. In addition, there were bombs and gases, acids and other corrosives. Turner demonstrated spring-loaded, steel-tipped wooden stakes that drove into the mechanical hearts of vampires. The push of a button would trigger enough explosive in the tip to blow their innards into so much slag and protoplasm.

Smiling at the impression he was making on the youth, Turner opened a wood-stained cabinet. "Here, Oliver. I've a gift for you. I *do* like you, and I only give these to people I care a great deal for." Inside the cabinet, perched on the top shelf, lay a pile of ten thick metal boxes about nine inches long, six wide. Turner reached up and slipped one out. "You know what this is?" he asked, leaning his chin somberly on his chest, scrunching up his dewlaps. He rapped the box slowly with a fingernail.

"Why, it's a box, Geoffrey."

"No—no, I mean what the box is made of!"

"Oh. Some sort of dark material, obviously heavy metal . . ."

"Lead, Oliver. Lead. It's to protect the bearer of the boxes from what's inside." The last two words Turner uttered in a sibilant whisper; a wonderful secret seemed to glimmer deep in his eyes.

"Which is?" Oliver asked, pondering why the man would want to make a gift of something dangerous.

"You can look at it briefly. There's no harm in that. Don't remove it for any length of time, unless you must. You can get the best effect in the dark." He shut the back door, closed the metal shutter by the controls, and switched off the overhead light. Darkness enveloped the interior. "Now, I'm going to open it for just a second or two." Oliver could hear the small squeak of hinges seldom used. He felt odd, as if involved in some magical rite.

In the dark, something began to shine. Oliver discerned the outlines of the box and Turner's hand against the brightening of that ghostly glow. Then the box was open. It held a cross, one that glowed white in the dark, against a dark velvet pad. The crucifix was almost as long and wide as the box, its nether end tapered to a knife point.

It shone like a star in the sky.

Turner held the box open just for a moment, then abruptly clacked it closed again, winking out the light. But the searing brightness lingered on Oliver's retina, a ghost-image of a burning, fiery-white cross in the darkness. A chill of some ghostly breeze touched his spine. He shivered with almost religious awe.

The light snapped back on.

Turner solemnly handed the closed box to Oliver. The man looked a bit green. A relapse of his hangover, thought Oliver.

"But I thought—I thought that only science and technology were worshiped in this van," Oliver objected, holding the metal box gingerly. "This is obviously a religious implement. What's it for?"

"The shape is merely for psychological purposes." Turner shuddered slightly, shaking off his momentary sickness. "The cross can serve as an effective, hilted knife, which is what is sometimes needed."

"You mean this is one of your weapons against the nightcreatures?"

"Yes. Most especially the vampires." Turner cleared a space on the cot, sat down, and patted a place for Oliver beside him. "You see, this is a very rare metal. It has radioactive properties—it gives off rays which make it glow. Now, when this metal is presented with a nightcreature—let's say a vampire—its rays dig deep into the thing's mechanism, doing much to mar its operation. If you stab a nightcreature in the proper place, you'll render it inoperative. But there *is* a cost. Frequent and prolonged use means exposure to human flesh—which causes sickness. Use it sparingly, only in emergencies."

"But why have you given me something so precious?" Oliver asked. "Why not keep it for yourself? Suppose you run out of the things, and need this one? I don't plan to encounter another nightcreature—*that's* for sure!" Oliver chuckled uncomfortably at his own joke.

"I'm going to ask you a question, Oliver," said the big man, looking him straight in the eye. "And I want you to think on your answer—don't give me one until you've thought it over thoroughly, all right?"

"Yes. But what?"

Turner held up a hand to silence him, then lowered it, placed his two thick hands together, and kneaded them. Staring down gloomily at the floor, he spoke in dark, sonorous tones:

"I am not a young man, Oliver. I am not as strong, as agile, as able as I once was, in my prime. Too, there is difficulty . . . there is—" He seemed to have difficulty pushing the words from his mouth. "In plain words—I have a problem. And this mission, this task of mine is almost too heavy, too much of a burden on my shoulders. I need help on this journey, Oliver. I need an assistant." He turned and looked at him soulfully, imploringly. "Will *you* come with me, Oliver Dolan?"

In the bowels of the mountain, the satyr leaned over its work, selectively soldering, rearranging wires, placing microcathodes, integrated circuits. To date, the bulk of the work on this Project had been effected in the genetic vats and by the mechanical processors. But this was a special project, an experimental Beast. It was the satyr's duty to check and recheck the Computer's product, and add the important odds and ends only nimble android fingers could handle.

The satyr was a low-sentience model, its half-flesh, half-machine mind molded specially for the kind of task on which it was engaged, with only the minimum of self-awareness to improve the reasoning faculties, so important in android prosthetic surgery. It was four feet tall. Its little horns gleamed in the bright strip-lit lab as its puckish face bobbed up and down, lost in the excitement it found in its duty, the enthusiasm with which it served its Master. Its hairy, nimble fingers danced among circuitry, pirouetted over plastoid and flesh, moving to the rhythms of the Prime Directive stored in its memory bank. In counterpoint were the pounding of the Beast's massive electric heart and the hiss of its breath, which sounded in the cavernous, antiseptic room like waves whooshing into a seashore, whispering out again.

This was the most important task ever set before the hoofed little fellow, and above all else it wished to do a good job, to please the Master. Pleasing Satan meant long hours immersed in pleasure-center stimulation.

While the satyr readjusted a tiny fm circuit buried deep in the new Beast's flesh, the ceiling speakers blared. The voice was Satan's. The little creature cringed, clicked backwards over the metal floor into a corner, and bowed its furry head. "I hear your call, Oh, Great One," it piped in a squeaky voice.

"Report on Project 39A34, Satyr 987W," the voice demanded imperiously.

"Currently correcting misplaced wiring. Also the fire expulsors in the jaws need corrective work." Its little mind wondered why the Master was so curious—he had never made such personal inquiries before. Perhaps the nature of the Beast? . . .

"The wings, the internal mechanism, the vital functions; are all these working properly?" The speakers rattled in their moorings.

"Splendidly, Master."

"Excellent. You will cease work, replace available body armor, and prepare for release of the Project."

"But . . . but, Master!" It blinked its watery eyes in consternation. "At least two days of work remain before it is perfect. Tests must be performed— And I have not received all of the necessary outer armor!"

"The wings work, do they not? The claws, the jaws, the vital destructive capacities are in good order? Is this not so, little one? Is there a flaw in you that this has not been accomplished yet, despite my priority instructions concerning the Beast? If so, perhaps a little internal correction is needed on your mechanism—" The voice became crackling thunder. "With a slight detour through your pain center for impertinence!"

"Yes, Master," the creature quavered. "All will be in readiness as soon as possible." Hastily, it returned to work. Soon, it knew, other servants would come and roll the unconscious Beast away to the Waking Chambers. It must be readied for them.

The satyr wondered why Satan needed the immense fire-breathing dragon, a project labored over for many years, so quickly.

FOUR

As Styx's great orange sun dipped toward evening, burnishing the tree leaves and lengthening the soft shadows, Oliver thought on Geoffrey Turner's request. As he pitched into the preparation for the Field Feasts, setting up the tables and chairs, he pondered the matter carefully.

"Oliver," the pudgy man had said, eyes molten with sincerity. "You are young, strong, vital. Not only is your assistance necessary, but just your presence would be enough to revivify this old hulk, imbue my frame with strength. Oliver, there is much that I can teach you. Much can be learned on this world, benighted as it is."

Much to be learned. The concept echoed in the youth's mind as he plumped down in a wooden lawn chair. His eyes looked over the spiked, ivy-webbed battlements of Fernwold Castle into the fresh blue of a clouded sky. Yes, there *must* be much to learn. Beyond the azure sky, Turner had said, were unimaginable distances—and yet they could be spanned by man-made machines to reach other worlds.

Oliver seldom ventured beyond the familiar environs of his duchy; the thought of other worlds was truly full of wonderful possibilities. And to learn the answers to questions for which the ministers had only vague mumbles, *that* would be something indeed.

Too, if Turner was not a madman, which hardly seemed possible, and there was truth to his cause, then it would be a noble task. A hard, dangerous labor, true, but if it succeeded as Turner hoped . . . "Why, lad, this world will be a place without fear! It will be as those who created it *intended* it to be, a world of happiness, of purpose. Think, Oliver Dolan, *think* of what Fernwold Castle would be like, without the constant threats of Nightworld.

"This will only be possible when the Oppressor has been vanquished, Oliver. But I will not make light of the magnitude of the task before me, and others of my League who are seeking the ship. It *is* hazardous. There will be more danger in the next month, if you accompany me, than you might know in a lifetime here, protected by your stone walls and your well-provisioned army. There will be brutes of terrible evil and strength stationed to hinder us. You will learn to *fight*. You will learn the use of my weapons.

"There is always the chance of death. And, should it come to pass, it won't be a comfortable death, believe me. However, all this is offset by the fact that it will be a noble undertaking, one that will give your life renewed meaning."

But he *had* meaning in his life! Was he not to succeed his father, would he not assume the governance of Fernwold's citizens?

"Yes, yes, certainly my lad. All very important. But think how much more you'll be doing for your people if you come with me. Think of what life would be for your *people*, if not for yourself, if we can rid Styx of this malignant creature Satan."

Playing soccer, a group of boisterous boys on the

daisy-dotted, fragrant greensward batted about a grass-stained white rubber ball joyfully, oblivious to the inner turmoil of Oliver Dolan.

To destroy Satan! That was a fine prospect, to be sure. To travel into the Nightworld and destroy God's principal Enemy. Was this possible? Surely Turner's quest would be a madman's journey. Use the bizarre weapons in Turner's van to eradicate Satan's fulsome nightcreatures on the way to some off-planet ship supposedly holding the weapons that could destroy Satan himself?

To that part of Oliver that held fast to the conservative religious beliefs of his upbringing, the notions were absurd. But strangely, to that part of him the idea of an adventure, a *holy* adventure, a quest of faith to destroy the Father of Lies, was also exciting. And, yes, *noble*.

His mind churned with indecision. What would his parents say? He would shirk his duties by undertaking an insane quest that might well spell his death, and bring damnation, too? Stepping into the Evil One's clutches, with such doubts as Turner had strewn in his thoughts, would surely be dangerous to his soul as well as to his mortal body.

Oliver just did not know.

The pang of indecision in him intensified his awareness of the messages of his senses: the savory aroma of roast chicken issuing from beneath the red-checked cloth of an old woman's basket; the delicate vermilion and violet wash of sunset draining from the sky; the bustling excitement of the youths jabbing at the ball and smacking into one another; the feel of the totality of the community, warmly and comfortably snuggled around him like a thick, old coat against the cold. How he loved all this. How could he risk losing it?

And what was this 'problem' Turner had spoken of? Surprised at the fat man's request, Oliver had neglected to ask. He would have to ask, soon, for Turner expected a reply to his invitation before bedtime. In the late morning, he would depart.

Whether with or without Oliver Dolan, Oliver had not decided.

He went into the castle to dress for the festivities.

Dusk curtained the sky. Glaring electric lamps and smoky torches glimmered, pushing up a ceiling of light in the night, when it happened.

"Yes, yes, quite true," Oliver said to the attentive, gowned girls clustered in an animated, perfumed pool of bows and frills by the badminton court's green turf. Dramatically, Oliver smote the air, pointing beyond the dark, brooding walls. The gesture shook the milky silk of his wide, ruffled goblet cuffs. An affirmative nod spilled carefully groomed curls onto his brow. "Out there, several hundred yards, a nightcreature *did* almost get me: a werewolf, to be exact." He put his hands to the long lapels of his dark blue serge topcoat which was cut off at the waist with long tails dropping to the tops of his lustrous brown leather boots. "And an awfully big one. I fell asleep by the stream and woke up—why, about this time yesterday, I'd say. Thing chased me a fearfully long time."

"Oh, Oliver!" cried a pretty young thing in an ankle-length mauve and green print muslin tea gown, decked with crisp scarlet ribbons, as she artfully placed the back of a petite hand to her mouth. "Weren't you *awfully* frightened?" Her dewy eyes widened and her bosom heaved slightly with excitement.

"Deuced right I was scared, and you'd be too, just to glimpse a *rendering* of the monster. And I saw it in the flesh, had the wretched thing on my heels!"

Oliver derived no little satisfaction from the reactions of the fetching young ladies settled about him like butterflies on a particularly attractive blossom. The social life of Fernwold was one of a young man's principle distractions; from the age of seventeen, Oliver had plunged into it with a vengeance. Handsome, mannerly, he had a way with the opposite sex that made him the envy of his comrades. He was thought a bit of a rake.

In actuality, he was rather frightened of women—just as he was frightened of his mother.

"And it was fearsome, if I say so myself! Ten feet tall at least. Claws as wide as any dagger hereabouts, curved like scythes. But did it catch me? Of course not." Oliver spoke in a clipped, understated tone to lend conviction to his hyperbole.

"Well, yes—of *course* I had to run, Fanny. But not before I gave the beast a good jab in the belly with a sharp stick, to let it know who it was dealing with! As a matter of fact, thanks to me that thing prowls the night no more!"

"You mean . . . you killed it?" Fanny asked. Her mouth hung open, revealing her surprise and two rows of imperfect, yellow teeth.

The pleated rose flounces of her gown swished against the luxuriant grass as she moved nearer, as though to catch every scrap of the tale. Suddenly Oliver felt giddy with her closeness and the faint scent of lavender that accompanied her.

"Well, let us say that I was of vital assistance in its—"

"Good evening, ladies," rumbled a heavy voice moving into the circle.

Angry at the interruption, Oliver swiveled his head. He blanched to learn that the voice belonged to Geoffrey Turner.

"Ah, Oliver! I see you are relating last evening's event to an enraptured audience." Turner's eyes gleamed mischievously at the young man. The corners of his mouth twitched into his dark black mustache. Yet the smile was not one of malice, but of friendly conspiracy. "Yes, ladies!" he boomed, slapping Oliver on the back with his left hand, while his other grasped a pint of brown frothy ale. "Oh, you would have been most thrilled at this young man's actions. T'would have quickened the pace of your hearts almost beyond endurance!" He looked at Oliver, and his corpulent face pulled back in contemplation. The atmosphere around him was redolent of yeasty brew and camaraderie. "Dear me, lad. I've interrupted you!"

"You mean, sir, that you were a witness to all that happened?" a young girl in pigtails asked, hugging herself with suspense.

"Yes indeed!" Turner cried, pushing back his handsome black topcoat to place his hand just below a natty double-breasted waistcoat. "Were it not for Oliver here, that infernal werewolf might well have gotten me!" Turner glanced at the surprised Oliver, giving him a surreptitious wink. "But I've interrupted the fellow. Do go on, dear boy. Or would you prefer to have me relate the tale?"

Oliver grinned. "Please do." The young ladies nodded eagerly. One spun a golden tasseled parasol nervously.

"Very well," Turner announced with a flourish of his free hand, ornamented tonight with rings of jade and silver. He took a pull of his drink, ahhed, and commenced with obvious relish, underscoring his words with broad gestures. "I had hoped to arrive at the gates of this good community before dusk, but alas, my maps were faulty, and I was a little late. Had not Oliver here drawn the werewolf's attention, *I* most likely would have been its unwary target. Now, as I was urging my steeds to a faster pace . . ."

A faint cry crackled through the air, like distant high-pitched thunder.

"Gracious," squeaked one of the girls through crooked teeth. "What was that?"

Turner shrugged. "Nothing of concern, my dear. As I was saying . . ."

The cry again, nearer. It had a strange, otherworldly quality, a combined hiss and roar.

Oliver rose to his tiptoes, as though trying to peer over the walls. "That *does* sound menacing. A nightcreature, no doubt."

The woman shivered at the word. Indeed, the entire crowd, formerly involved in chatter, play, eating, and laughing, suddenly grew quiet and gazed nervously in the direction from which the sound originated. The air suddenly seemed charged with electricity.

"Now, now," Turner said. "No need to be alarmed. I've dealt with nightcreatures for some time, and I've yet to encounter one who's topped the wall of a fortified community. And *these* walls, why they're quite splendid, taller than most, you know. Nothing to fear— yes, yes, the others seem to realize that, too—see, they've gone about their enjoyment of this evening as we should. As I was saying . . ."

A scream of fright caused the big man to start, tilting his top hat over his eyes. Another scream erupted in its wake.

Whipping his head around, Oliver could scarce keep in his breath. A winged creature slanted downward from the sky, four clawed feet outstretched, preparing to land on the turf where hundreds of people congregated.

"Good God," said Turner in an awed voice, righting his hat. He lost his hold on the mug, which clunked to the grass, splashing its ale over his neatly creased pants leg. "A dragon. A flying dragon—with a wingspan of, why it must be over forty feet!" he whispered, between his teeth. "Never knew Nicholas was making this sort of thing—never knew the Computer had the facilities."

The dragon, gliding closer now, shrilled a dreadful cry of blood-lust. The creature had wings like those of a giant bat—leathery, black and taut over bulging bones. Its long, scaly, green body was prototypical dragon with a long, whipping tail. The huge head was mostly mouth and sword-length teeth. Above that, eyes the size of cannon balls rolled about their sockets, jumped from group to group, eyeing all malevolently.

"Heavens, Oliver! Look!" Turner cried. "See—the thing's not even completed yet—examine its underbelly . . . there, lad. You can see the machinery!"

Indeed, Oliver could see that little skin covered its underside—in fact, he noticed other segments of the winged beast similarly lacking in armor; behind the purpled ear on its right, along its sharp, spined back, and just left of its long serpent's throat, Oliver could make out the blink of lights within the beast behind the naked flesh.

Then the dragon landed in a clearing just yards from the astounded townspeople, tearing up chunks of the green with its wide-spread claws as it settled. The flapping of its ungainly wings blew up dirt and dust. At first the beast looked as though it might tilt over, but it regained its balance and folded its wings back along its body, hiding some of its armorless sections. A foul odor, rot laced with rancid oil, gusted in its vanguard assault on Oliver's senses.

The thing reared back its mammoth head, gazed upon the frightened townsfolk with its lizard-face, and opened its maw. A long stream of fire enveloped the nearest group of people, some dozen men and women, giving the victims no opportunity to cry out in panic or pain before their immolation.

The others screamed, though, once their initial shock had dissipated. One of the girls in Oliver's group turned and ran. Others scrambled after her, tripping and falling in their breakneck dash.

"Halt!" thundered a tremendous voice. Oliver, who was about to turn and seek shelter himself, noted it was the dragon that spoke. "Run, people, and I'll destroy you all with pleasure." The beast's mouth opened and shut, wisps of fetid oily smoke rising about its face like sinister black mustaches. "Stop, and I'll spare you all—save the man I seek, who skulks within these walls."

Those fleeing stopped in supernatural dread, obeying.

The ministers dropped to their knees, praying for divine intervention. Geoffrey Turner leaned toward Oliver. "It's me he's after, lad," he said somberly. "There's but one hope. You go stall it. The voice is Satan's. He's talking through a loudspeaker implanted in the dragon's mouth. I'll return in a moment—tell it that."

"But it will kill me!" Oliver objected, grabbing at

the fat man's coat, "just like—just like it killed those poor people!"

"No, no, Satan's proud, boastful. Make him talk. Tell him I'll give myself up, that I'm being sought, being brought for him. Take courage, lad. Show me of what stuff you're made." So saying, he abruptly turned and snuck into the crowd.

"I seek Geoffrey Turner!" the dragon snarled in its heart-chilling voice. "Bring this man before me, bring Geoffrey Turner to me, and I shall harm no more of you, nor shall I return! He is here, that I know. He is here, and I shall find him if I have to burn down your houses, and rip apart your castle stone by stone!"

Oliver took a deep breath, voiced a quiet prayer, and ran out into the clearing between the cowering crowd and the swaying, growling dragon. Halting some ten yards from the creature, he turned his face upwards, stood straight and firm. The stench here was overpowering. Cinders still flecked the air.

"You are not Turner!" said the dragon. Its mouth widened as though to loose another flame.

"No—wait!" Oliver cried desperately, lifting a halting hand. "Turner is being sought by my soldiers at this very moment. I have ordered them to drag him here. The coward is no friend of ours, and we'll be happy to let you have him."

The dragon snaked its head closer to obtain a better view of this brave, dandified young man. "Who are you, boy, to give such orders?"

"I, Satan, am Oliver Dolan, second in command of the Army of Fernwold by right of heritage."

"Ah, you know who controls this beast then. You know who I am, who is truly speaking at the moment." The gargantuan eyes glittered.

"Yes, and I quake in my boots to hear your magnificent voice!" cried Oliver, bending into a bow from the waist. "Your greatness and fearsomeness is legend throughout the world. Your creatures plague us, your evil holds us, and it is only by the grace of God that we are not entirely in your power. I am truly awed at the mere resonance of your voice, to say nothing of the physical might of your creation."

The dragon seemed to take pleasure in Oliver's language of obeisance. Its wings unfurled a little, flapped as though preening itself, whipping up a wind that blew Oliver's hair and coattails about, and tugged at his pale blue cravat.

"And well you should be impressed by my might, petty human," it hissed, obviously delighted. "Well you should heed my words. But you say this bane of mine, this Geoffrey Turner, is being brought to me?"

"A matter of moments and he will be at your disposal," the youth said. The audible quaver in his voice was not difficult to affect. "In the meantime, might I add, Satan, that we mere mortals are seldom privileged with a direct visitation by your majesty—even if it is from a distance, as it were. How is it this Turner fellow is of such importance to you, that you seek him in this incredible guise?"

"Why should I deign to answer your trifling questions, mortal?" the dragon snarled. It spat a spurt of fire down to char the grass not two yards from Oliver's feet. The youth grimaced at the terrific heat, but stood still. The acrid smoke tickled his nostrils.

"We offer no resistance, Satan," he responded. "We realize and appreciate the scope and might of your all-encompassing power. I wish merely to understand its nature. Surely to impart this to us would not deplete your glory, indeed, it would give my people a greater recognition of your awesomeness."

"They shall all worship *me* one of these days," Satan declared, hoisting its left set of claws and squeezing them together like a fist. "*Me.* Not some airy nothing of a God in the Heavens who heeds them not. Do you understand that?"

Where was Turner? Oliver could not continue much longer; it took every bit of his courage to muster words before the behemoth. How long his words would last he had no way of knowing.

"That is yet to be seen, Father of Evil. But we do

understand the possibility." His underarms sopped with prickly perspiration, his brow ran with cold, clammy sweat. "However, we are not aware of the totality of your evil, spread across this world. Tell me this, then— Geoffrey Turner has told us that you are not a super- natural entity at all—that you are perhaps only a mad machine, creating chaos on this world that was once part of an empire of many worlds. Is this so?"

"Nonsense!" the dragon roared, wisps of smoke curl- ing from its nostrils. "The man speaks absurdities. He reflects the senility of the Enemy whom he serves! I was an angel in heaven, and chose to establish a base here on Styx—I did not care for the way my Enemy was running things. Once I rule the entirety of this world, I shall storm the gates of Heaven, and from there rule the Universe, which is my destiny!"

"According to our beliefs, you were *thrown* from Heaven by God along with fellow prideful angels." Oliver did not care much for the course this conver- sation was taking; he might well arouse the thing's ire— and fire. But he could think of nothing more to say— and silence would surely try Satan's patience. A quick glance about him told Oliver that the crowd was yet standing still, stunned as the scene unfolded—and that there was no sign of Turner.

A doubt flickered, then burst into flame. Had the man run for his life? Had he left Oliver and his people to fend for themselves?

His attention was brought back to the dragon by its reaction to his last statement: "Your beliefs lie, and shall be changed as soon as I rule this world!" Advanc- ing, it loomed near, hooked Oliver's coat with a claw, lifting him upward. The sharp, dirt-stained claw, Oliver could see now, was steel. It skewered the top of his coat jaggedly, and the frock coat's seams slowly ripped beneath Oliver's weight. The metal claw against his bare skin was as cold as death. "Why do you anger me, petty one?" The dragon's noxious breath seemed composed of equal parts gasoline and decomposed meat fumes. Oliver was so close, he could detect bits of meaty gristle wedged between the monster's pointed, yellowed teeth. Suddenly, the creature tossed him contemptuously away, tearing the coat to rags. Oliver bumped so hard on his rear, the momentum somersaulted him over into a disheveled, stunned scatter of arms and legs amidst the cushioning grass. "I think you are stalling me. This I will not tolerate. You will die for your impudence."

The dragon's head loomed closer hideously. The mouth gaped, yawning incredibly wide. Oliver braced himself for a fiery death.

Suddenly a tremendous explosion hurled Oliver head over heels. He barely clung to consciousness as the force propelled him along the ground. Rocking to a stop, he gazed up, and was startled by what he saw.

Now scorched brown, the dragon's jaw dripped a thick red ichor. From its nostrils smoke and random flames billowed. The voice within sputtered and screamed in anger. Obviously it had no further use of the jaw, a ruined twisted mess.

What had happened?

Oliver climbed shakily to his feet. However, poised to run for his life, he noted movement to his right.

Turning back, he faced Satan's dragon once more, and screamed hoarsely, the taste of fear bitter in his mouth. "Here he comes!" He pointed to his left, to divert the creature's attention. "Here comes Geoffrey Turner, Satan!"

Even though its fire-breathing faculties were destroyed, the remainder of the beast still seemed to be operable. Following Oliver's gesture, the dragon's neck turned—and therefore it did not immediately notice what Oliver had seen.

Turner's van, horseless, whisked rapidly toward the beast. Geoffrey Turner *had* kept his word. Expectation tingled in Oliver.

The big wheeled box was on course to ram the dragon, but the axles rattled as it neared, attracting the beast's attention. The dragon swung its bloody head around and adjusted its stance to brace for the collision, able to spread its wings to flap away.

But too late.

The heavy vehicle barreled into the beast's left wing, snapping it. The crack echoed about the walls and buildings like the voice of a giant whip. The broken wing crumpled and the van plowed directly into the dragon's side. With a sickening crunch, the thing toppled.

The dragon loosed a horrendous roar, a mixture of anger and agony. Its thick tail lashed violently against Turner's van and the mighty claws gashed long rents in the wood veneer. Van and dragon skidded a full ten yards before sliding to a halt.

The van's wheels began to rotate backward, but the van did not move. Turner was trying to back up, and again smash into the dragon. But the beast held the van fast, claws dug deep into the wood, tail curled around the chassis.

"All right, men!" erupted a cry from behind him. "Fire at will!" Oliver turned. Some thirty armed Fernwold soldiers raised their rifles. Giving orders was his father.

The ancient rifles cracked and popped, splattering bullets into the dragon. Some bullets bounced off its scales, but others ripped through the unarmored portions of the dragon's body. Gouts of blood spurted. An eye exploded into crystalline powder. Blood leaked profusely from the cavity.

Careful not to place himself in the line of fire, Oliver hustled back.

"Father," he cried. "Turner's in that van!"

Tears streamed down the man's ashen face. He reloaded his rifle. The scent of spent gun powder charged the air. "He can fend for himself. I just want that beast destroyed, before it harms others."

Oliver could see there would be no discussion of tactics with his father—the man was in a towering rage. If the dragon was not killed soon, it might well crush the van, *and* Turner, thus succeeding in its mission. A soldier, not in uniform, had just reloaded his rifle. Oliver pounced upon him, tore it away, and dashed

toward the deadlocked machines. The soldier's cries
drew Viscount Dolan's attention. He yelled to his son,
but to no avail.

Oliver knew that to still the beast, the bullet had to
be fired at close range. He remembered Turner had
destroyed the werewolf by upsetting its internal mechanisms. If he could do the same with a properly placed
bullet, then there was hope for the man, and the van.

Moving to the blind side of the maddened beast, he
scanned the length of its body. He had observed a patch
of unprotected surface—yes, there, exposed just below
the wing.

Nearing as close as he dared, Oliver aimed at the
blinking lights dimly visible through the beast's translucent covering.

And squeezed off the bullet.

Metal and glass smashed with hollow tinkles and
violent explosions. Sparks flew through the opening and
a hint of noisome smoke, small clouds of it, billowed
from the machinery. A flame flickered, and another,
like red tongues from a mouth.

The dragon jerked. Spasming, it unhooked its claws
from the van. The tail whipped out of control, like a
wriggling serpent.

Freed, the van rapidly backed well away from the
dragon, now contorting its broken body insanely.

Oliver sprinted away and called to the soldiers.
"Closer! Continue your fire!"

The rear doors of the van split open and Turner's
obese form tumbled out, shaken. He wobbled toward
the soldiers, all the while staring at the twitching form
of the defeated dragon. "Close," he muttered. "Very
close." He stepped forward, and cupped his hands to
his mouth. "So much for your spanking new monsters,
Satan," he cried. "So much for your incredible power!"

Flames now spouted from various apertures in the
beast's body armor. It should have been finished. And
yet, incredibly, the body stilled its thrashings, save for
its head, which swiveled about to regard Turner with
its one good eye. "Your soul shall yet be mine, fat

fool," Satan's voice crackled. "And your body I shall spit with wire. I shall sizzle the fat from it in the depths—"

An explosion burst the dragon, throwing fiery bits into the night sky. The head tumbled and lay still on the blackened ground.

The people, still stunned, milled about, astonished. Members of the other Field Feast sites watched from the roads, open-mouthed.

Oliver approached his father, who hugged him. "Had I not hit the beast properly," said Lord Dolan, tears still in his eyes. "Had I not fired into its mouth—" The familiar, homey smell about the Viscount soothed Oliver's nerves.

"You caused the mouth to malfunction, Father?"

"I thought bullets would not harm it—but I was wrong," said the tall man. "Thank God, I directed rifles be obtained anyway. And thank Him that He directed the aim of my rifle, or you would be as dead as your mother, Oliver."

"My mother?" said Oliver, disbelievingly.

"Yes," said the Viscount, in a choking voice. "She was killed in the beast's first fire-blast."

The mountain itself seemed to quake with Satan's fury.

The satyr mechanic was wakened from its rest, and dragged by two apprentice demons to the depths of the steel-walled Hell, to stand before the creature who called itself Satan. Fearful, the satyr trembled at the terrible countenance of its Master.

"I have just severed the radio link with my dragon, furry one. Do you know what happened?" the man-thing asked from its murmuring vat.

"A successful mission, I trust, Great One," squealed the goat-man, shaking with terror.

"No. It was not successful!" bellowed the voice. "It was humiliating—and should not have been. The dragon should have been indestructible."

"But Master, it would have been, if I had had sufficient time to work—"

"Silence! I will not countenance impudence. I see I have placed too much self-awareness in your model. That will be corrected in your fellows. The fire-breathing mechanism, furry one, was to have been shielded. Measures were to have been taken to prevent an explosion of the gases, should a malfunction occur. And the shielding along the body? What about that? It was to be my most terrible nightcreature, a prototype of many such beasts to spread horror amongst the sequestered humans in their wretched, stone-walled shelters."

"But Satan, I did mention . . ."

"Enough of this. There is no excuse. You shall be

dismantled, *furry-one—but not until you undergo tor-ture to recompense for my extreme frustration."*

Demons hauled the little goat-man from the chamber.

Another demon separated itself from the shadows, and scrabbled out into the smoky pungent torchlight, dragging long arms along the floor.

"You were sent in search of the fallen vessel, is this not true?"

"Yes, Master," it said. "As reported, we have narrowed the search area and expect to locate the space-craft in a matter of days. I have returned for instructions as to what you wish done, once it is discovered."

"I shall arm you with sufficient means," said Satan. "I want the thing destroyed as soon as possible, along with any passengers it may contain."

FIVE

❖━❖━❖━❖━❖━❖━❖━❖━❖━❖━❖━❖━❖

THE sun rose, but the mourning had already begun.
Great as his grief was, Oliver kept himself too busy
to allow it to take total sway. For he was helping Geoffrey Turner to prepare for embarkation from Fernwold.
And he was making ready to accompany the man.

All night workmen and carpenters had labored to
repair the superficial damage the dragon had wreaked
upon the van, while an extension cord plugged into the
community's power supply recharged the vehicle's batteries. Ample provisions—dried meats and vegetables,
fresh fruit, spirits and wine—were stocked in Turner's
cupboards. Everything possible was done to help the
man. The evening's incident had brought the truth of
their precarious situation to Viscount Dolan. Once the
wreckage of the dragon-android was cool, Turner poked
through it, explaining the functions of various charred
mechanisms to the stunned ruler of Fernwold. Dolan,
afterward, agreed that everything possible should be
done to destroy Satan. He extended his whole-hearted
approval to Turner's mission.

Dolan did not know, then, that he would be giving a son to the cause as well.

After he finally went to bed, Oliver had not slept well.

Early in the morning, he went to Turner's chambers, awakened the man, and informed him that he would gratefully accept the chance to revenge his mother's death and relieve Styx of this evil creature.

Then he went to his father, but Viscount Dolan was not in his sleeping quarters.

As he passed the den, Oliver noticed an arm draped over the side of the over-stuffed, high-backed chair fronting the burnt-out hearth. Its hand held an empty bottle of spirits.

"Father?" Oliver said, moving over the thick brown rug and settling quietly into the adjacent chair. "Father, I have to talk to you."

Viscount Dolan's blood-shot, baggy eyes fluttered half-open, looked out blearily from a puffy, stubbled face. His first reaction to consciousness was to raise the bottle to his lips. Finding that it was dry, he tossed it into the fireplace. The sound of crashing glass seemed to bring him to his senses. He groaned.

"Father? Are you all right? I have to talk to you."

Lord Dolan leaned his cheek into an open palm, rubbed his face with shaky hand, sighed. "Gone," he muttered. "A flash of fire, and she's gone, forever."

A tear dripped from Oliver's eye. He smudged the warm wetness away. No trace of emotion reached his voice. "I mean to see that her death is not meaningless, Father," he announced quietly. "Geoffrey Turner has invited me to accompany him in search of the means to destroy Satan."

Dolan stared at his son impassionately through red eyes. "And you've accepted?"

"I have to. I shall never forgive myself if I forego the opportunity."

The Viscount nodded. The drooping locks of his hair barely swayed. "So, I am to lose you to the night-creatures after all."

"You can't stop me from going, Father. I'm old enough to make my own decisions. If I'm killed, then the succession goes to cousin Eric, who is every bit as good as I. Yes, Father. I'm going, and I mean to return."

Viscount Dolan averted his somber gaze. "Perhaps. I pray so. I'll not try to stop you. I understand. I think . . . if *I* could go, with the possibility of bringing relief to this accursed world, I would." He closed his eyes. "You'll be leaving this morning, then?"

"Yes. As soon as the van is repaired. I'll not be here for the funeral."

"You'll go with my blessings. Funerals are meaningless." Clasping his hands, he let his eyes open fully, and stared at his son. "Oliver, all my life has been occupied by my domain, and my wife. I've given you little attention, little love, son. I realized that last night, about four inches into the bottle. I told myself I'd make that up to you. Now, perhaps I won't get a chance to. That grieves me, Oliver, perhaps as much as your mother's terrible passing. I'm sorry that I've not been the best of fathers, Oliver." He rested his chin on his chest silently.

Rising, Oliver placed a hand on his shoulder. "Not true, sir. Not true."

He squeezed the sagging, burdened shoulder briefly, turned, and stepped quietly from the room.

The nearest community was less than a day's ride, so Turner retrieved his team from the royal stables.

"We'll give them to the Blassingame community, lad, and commence from there under the van's power. We'll have to take shelter in it a few times from there forward, and I don't want the poor beasts torn to bits by nightcreatures."

They set out on the rough, rutted highway just before the sun reached its zenith in a cloudless sky. Oliver sat on the newly refurbished front seat of the van, beside Turner.

The frenzied claws of the dragon had ripped much of the wood from the metal frame of the coach. Fern-

wold's carpenters had done wonders. Ripping off the
rest of the scarred wood, they had quickly crafted a
new walnut covering, making the van more elegant
than it had been when first assembled. Electric lanterns
rose from each of the four upper corners. Tassels
fringed the ornate roof. On the rear was carved the
sign of the cross, symbolic to Fernwoldian minds of the
mission of Geoffrey Turner.

Turner assumed the reins for the first leg of the journey. Oliver was content to sit beside him, jiggling occasionally when the carriage hit holes or bumps, and staring resolutely ahead, intent on his purpose.

The autumnal countryside was frantic with colors,
odors, and subtle textures, as though the current gen-
eration of flora, dying toward winter, was vibrantly
seizing its last days to expire with a joy it had never
known in its youthful spring and lazy, mature summer.
Stands of beech, elm, ash, birch, and poplar marched
along the roadway, splashed with ochers, reds, silvers,
and light blues, spotted here and there with the eternal
emerald of conifer copses.

Gray gorse and thorny thickets wrapped about the
browning bark of the trees, spilling over occasionally
to flood the ancient road. Weeds populated most of the
ill-maintained byway, hiding the treacherous holes and
bumps.

The air was thick with perfumed decay, laced with
the scents of gay wildflowers sprouting as though summer still hung in the branches nodding overhead.

The animals of the land, when visible from Oliver's
jostling perch on top of the van, seemed in a flurry of
activity. Gray squirrels bounced in cheerful, hasty nut-
hunts. Rabbits, frightened by the strident squeakings of
the van's suspension, bounced in gray and white flashes
to the shelter of scrub where, safe, they twitched their
whiskers and pink noses in curiosity at the mammoth
intruder into their leafy domain. Birds fluttered frantically from tree to tree. Robins, starlings, and sparrows
scolded the wheeled monster as it lumbered in their
midst, pulled by the pair of patient, russet-brown

horses, bearing Oliver and Turner to their uncertain fates.

For a long while they said nothing.

Soon after the start of their journey, Turner had plucked a long-stemmed jet pipe from a deep pocket of his sepia frock-coat. He mashed curious blends of tobacco and dull-green weeds into its bowl, and sucked on the pungent brown fumes with relish, contemplating. Then Turner broke the silence. "Must be hard for a young lad to lose his mother. I want to say how sorry I am, Oliver. This has been preying on my mind since last night—if I hadn't come to Fernwold, neither would Satan's dragonoid have come. I feel at fault. If you harbor any resentment, please forgive me." Turner repositioned the pipe stem, clenching it morosely between white molars.

The abrupt statement startled the youth from his brown study. He considered, then said, "That really doesn't make sense. By the same token, if you'd not saved me from that werewolf, chances are you'd have left the following morning, and the dragon would not have been sent. Fate is fate, Geoffrey, what happens, happens. It's not your fault, nor mine. The fault belongs entirely to Satan, and I mean to see that he pays."

"All the same, I do feel rather badly about the whole thing."

"Well, don't," Oliver commanded brusquely. "Let's just concentrate on the journey ahead."

"Good," Turner said, a small smile provoking dimples in his rosy cheeks. "Happy that's settled. For a while, I thought that having you aboard this cruise would be as bad as being alone."

"I'm sorry, sir—I mean, Geoffrey. But you can't blame me for my quiet mood."

"Not blaming you at all, Oliver."

"You know, Geoffrey, I know very little about you. Only this business about you being part of HOPE. Exactly where *do* you come from?"

The horse-drawn van was nearing a clump of low, bulky, fir tree covered hills. Here, the road dipped and rose. At a rise, overlooking a vast virgin forest, principally composed of firs and cypresses, Turner began speaking of his past.

The landmass of the planet consisted of one single continent that wrapped its variably thick self about the world, the salt sea ribboning it like a never-ending river. Hence the name Styx—the name of the mythical river leading to the Greek underworld. Turner claimed to be from a section of the vast continent farther south, closer by sea than by land. As a young man, he told Oliver, he had been a scholar studying for ordination in the church. But his nimble mind hungered for answers to questions his teachers shunned. One day, he had encountered an old, old man who told him about the Holy Order for the Preservation of the Empire. His curiosity piqued, he sallied forth seeking the fortified castle where HOPE maintained its headquarters.

"It was quite far to the north, dear boy, *quite* far," the fat man intoned gravely. "I had many a brush with death, believe me. This world is far from hospitable to long-term travelers. Finally, after many wrong turns and faulty directions, close to three months after I set out, I arrived at a singularly unusual manse, not at all like the general run of those favored by most of the communities of this world."

It seemed that some rapping at the gates brought forth a number of strangely robed men bearing unusual weapons. After determining that the supplicant was not a minion of Satan trying to infiltrate their ranks, they passed Turner through the gates and allowed him to join their number. For fully twenty years Turner had reveled in the well-stocked libraries of the institute. Often, along with others of the Order, he ventured out on missions, destroying nightcreatures plaguing surrounding communities.

"Actually, half the battle was convincing the common people that the nightcreatures were killable. You saw that your father's bullets, placed properly, did a pretty good job on that dragon, right? The most important

mission of HOPE relating to the other denizens of
Styx has been education on self-defense. If the people
won't believe the true origin of the nightcreatures, the
least we can teach them is how to kill the buggers!"

Turner hurrumphed and clenched the reins tightly in
his fists.

Late afternoon found them atop a rise, before the
barbican and spires of Blassingame, a middling town
situated on the south bank of a wide, muddy river.

Oliver knew the Viscount of the community, one
Sampson Napper, quite well from the occasional visits
he and Napper had made between Blassingame and
Fernwold. So it was that when they arrived at the point-
groined Norman gates of the hold and identified themselves to the satisfaction of the gate-house guards, the
portcullis was raised and they were welcomed. Napper
hosted them a sumptuous dinner of roast quail and wild
duck and in turn received their tale, and the purpose
of their travels. He shook his gray-haired head and
grumbled pessimistically that they would be destroyed
by the supernatural legions of Satan, but offered little
else by way of comment. Geoffrey Turner asked if tales
of a large ship landing on Styx had filtered to the ministers of Blassingame. But no, responded Napper. Nothing.

Oliver and Turner were provided with comfortable,
airy rooms for the night. In the morning they were given
a large, filling breakfast of eggs, scones, and strawberry
marmalade. Upon learning that the nearest community
in the direction he wished to go was a day's ride on a
fast horse, and could not be covered in similar time
in a van drawn by horses, Turner abandoned his animals in Blassingame as promised.

Much to the amazement of the townsfolk who saw
the sight, they drove the horseless van away, with no
apparent driver in view.

Oliver felt curious riding in such a manner. Turner
was bent intently over the controls, and a steady hum
emanated from the compact electric engines. But in a
few hours he grew accustomed to the change, and spent

the majority of the day absorbed in a book his companion insisted he study. A text printed by HOPE, it dealt with the destruction of various nightcreatures. The volume contained schematics of the beasts' inner workings, which Oliver could not comprehend at all. But he did understand the simple descriptions of the weak points of the various and sundry beast-machines that roamed the night.

"There is one question that is not answered by all this," Oliver said, looking up from where he sat.

"And what is that?" Turner asked, eyes trained on the road. He kept the vehicle at a pace not much faster than it went when drawn by horses, partly to conserve power, partly to mitigate the harmful effects of speed over the many pits and bumps in the road.

"I understand now that you are right; that the forces with which we deal are basically natural and explainable. I cling to my basic beliefs as to the reason for their existence, but I accept what you have shown and told me."

"Excellent, my lad! You're almost there."

"Wait a moment," Oliver replied. "I'm not finished. What I don't understand is, if Satan himself is perhaps merely a man in control of machinery, and if these monsters of flesh and metal are only what you say they are, why then do they operate under spiritual and supernatural conditions? Why, if they are as solid and substantial, of the same basic elements as you or I and this van, why are they not able to go about by day? Why are they limited to the night, the dark?"

"Ah, you've put your finger on a question the Order has asked itself for a very long time, a *very* long time. If this madman wants the world entirely, and he has the power to make all humans his slaves, why doesn't he do it? At the very least, why can't he terrorize the day as he does the night?"

"Perhaps because he is restricted by the laws of God," ventured Oliver. "Because, although he works by physical means, he is actually warring with the forces of light, the spiritual armies of our Lord and Savior."

"Perhaps. I'd very much like to believe that, but I fear that *this* would-be clergyman has turned skeptic. No, consider my theory first.

"I believe I've mentioned that HOPE believes this Satan to be quite mad—and a man, not a fallen angel. Our theory is that not only does he act and operate like Satan, but he really thinks he *is* Satan. He suffers from megalomania."

"But Geoffrey, he *is* Satan. How can he model himself on himself?"

"Yes, and here is where background knowledge proves valuable, facts I've not yet provided you.

"The religion of the people of Styx is Christianity, indeed, but a vague, muddled Christianity in the sense that the actual historical origins are fuzzy—assumed rather than documented. I put this to you, Oliver: Christianity did not begin on this world."

"But—but that's impossible!"

"Not at all, if you accept the historical facts of the creation of Styx, instead of calling them myths as your father did. The entirety of this Empire I spoke of before, began on one planet, the original home of mankind. It was known by various names, among them Terra, Telluria, or simply the rather humorous name of 'Earth'."

"Pah!" Oliver exclaimed. "You might as well call it 'Dirt'!"

Turner lifted a hand from the control wheel. "Be that as it may, it was Earth on which Christianity began, long before the advent of travel across the great voids that separate the worlds of the galaxy. We have books to prove this. Many such books reflect the beliefs of Christianity. In much the form of your own beliefs, Christianity has changed little over the years, for it *is* a morally solid and compelling rationalization of the Universe. In its more rudimentary versions, stocked with many anthropomorphisms and a more or less dualistic Earth-centered view of the Universe, the adversary of God was one of his angels, Satan, who ruled over the creatures and demons of darkness as *our* Satan rules over his creations."

"You still haven't answered my question," Oliver interjected impatiently.

"A moment," said Turner, cutting the wheel hard to avoid an obstacle in the road. "Right. It is the theory of HOPE that Satan, in his desire to identify himself completely with his Earthly namesake, has not only copied the powers ascribed to the medieval Satan of long-ago Earth, he has also adopted his limitations. In order for him to be evil, there must be good in the world with which to battle. In other words, there is absolutely no physical reason why the beasts do not also roam by day. It is all mental—and in the mind of Satan. This is one of the reasons I was so surprised that he had a dragon built, and flew it over the walls of Fernwold. Such an action bends the rules Satan has established for himself, and means he wants me dead, desperately. Why, I don't know. Perhaps he's seeking others of HOPE as well. Perhaps he realizes that there is danger to him if we find the fallen spaceship and its passengers before he does."

"Are you telling me, Geoffrey, that all these centuries of darkness and misery have been because of a crazy *game* this thing is playing with us?"

"It's not a game to him, it's deadly serious. We're lucky he has kept himself in check by his own rules, or he would surely control the entirety of this world."

"That just doesn't make sense."

"Certainly it does. Take for example, your father's thinking his bullet couldn't really harm the dragon. Did he base that belief on empirical evidence? No, it was superstition, a firm belief that Satan's nightcreatures are almost impervious to harm from humans." He picked up a bottle of wine he had been nipping at all day, took a gulp of the red stuff. "Such is the case with Satan. He's really convinced himself that his creatures will not work in the daytime—that the sun's rays will harm them. The curious factor in this whole affair is that our principal aid in this journey, in our continual battle against Satan, is a solid belief in God and His power."

"But—" Oliver objected.

Turner took his eyes from the road a moment, pointed a forefinger at Oliver. "Not *our* belief—*Satan's* belief."

"Satan believes in God, just as I do?"

The fat man returned to his driving. "If there is no God of Christianity, why there would be no cause for a Satan, right?"

"You mean in order for this creature to believe that he is actually the fallen archangel, Satan, he must believe that there is a God he once served, and now opposes?"

"Correct. His chief purpose in existence, as was the original Satan's, is to pervert the good things that the Christian God has created, and to ultimately control this world, and God's heaven."

Oliver grew silent, and thoughtful.

The van sped on, the ever-changing landscape unfolding its wealth of florid variety, hills, mountains, rivers and valleys which the parti-colored road wound through.

They traveled several days without incident. During this time, Turner taught Oliver how to operate the van, no easy assignment. At first it was frightening for the lad to handle the controls of a mechanism he understood so poorly, to feel power throb beneath him, to manipulate that energy so as to keep the vehicle moving at the correct rate of speed in the proper direction.

"It's simple," Turner had explained. "You'll get the feel of the wheel soon enough. The pressure exerted on the pedal under your right foot moderates the flow of electricity from batteries to engine, and hence the speed. Any problems you have are easily handled with one of these buttons before you—I'll explain their functions later."

On the afternoon of their third day of travel, Turner pronounced his pleasure at Oliver's solo driving, and promptly retired with a wine bottle to his cot. That bottle troubled Oliver, for Turner had been pulling at it all afternoon, and he had slurped liquor long into the previous evening.

But the other things in his mind were troubling as well, as the van ate up the distance slowly but surely along the winding, forest-flanked ribbon of road that stretched out into the distance. His bravado, that earnest desire for revenge which had set him on the mission was gradually draining, leaving the weaker part of his personality in control. The meekness basic to Oliver Dolan was reasserting itself. Fear began to gnaw.

All right. So this Satan was not the spiritual Satan. That did not mean that he was not a front for the *real* arch-demon.

And even if there was no spiritual danger in challenging these forces of darkness, there was still the possibility of horrible, painful death looming huge in his mind, peering up beast-like from the pit of his subconscious fears.

Late afternoon found the van struggling up grades and rolling down slopes in a hilly area in which maple trees predominated. As the van crackled through the dead brown leaves covering the roadbed, Oliver mused darkly. His inattention almost caused him to collide with the woman trying to attract his attention.

Her clothes were torn, her pale face scratched and bloody.

Feebly waving an arm, she stood quivering in the middle of the road like a wounded deer, imploring aid.

SIX

><<=><=><=><=><=><=><=><=><=><=><=><=><=><=><

OLIVER lifted his foot from the rubber-sheathed accelerator and applied the brakes. He stared at the woman staggering toward the van, as it halted.

She wore a tattered gray riding skirt, and a ragged fawn cape, over an unkempt white satin blouse. The long, blonde hair visible beneath her cream and red bonnet was tousled, and bits of dead brown leaves clung to it. Her lips moved, but Oliver could not hear what she said.

"Geoffrey!" he cried. "Wake up. There's someone up ahead. A woman, and she's hurt."

"What's that?" Turner's voice growled from the rear. Boots thudded on the steel floor, and Oliver's hirsute companion peered intently over his shoulder through the windshield. Turner groggily wiped the sleep from his eyes and renewed the stare, clearer this time.

The woman stumbled, caught herself, then collapsed into a heap of ragged clothing.

"Well, what are we standing here for?" Turner bellowed as much to himself as to his associate. He tugged

Oliver's shirt sleeve, pivoted, and was soon muttering indistinctly over the opening apparatus. The rear door squeaked as it gave way. Turner pounded to the ground, and bounded around the van. Jumping out the door, Oliver was close on his heels, dashing into the brisk autumn air.

Hands under her arms and knees, they carried the young woman back to the van. They carefully eased her into the van and placed her on the cot. Upon contact with the soft padding, her lolling arms stiffened, straightened, and gripped Turner's neatly-pressed lapels. Opening her eyes, she immediately realized that the men meant only to help. She relaxed, dropped her head to the mussed pillow, mumbling broken phrases: "Dear me . . . sorry to trouble you . . . I must look a fright . . . really not badly off . . . just a bit dazed . . . no need to trouble yourselves."

"She's all right," Turner remarked after a thorough sensor-scan of her body and face. "No broken bones. A few scratches here and there—and a nasty gash on her head." Moving to a cabinet, he clunked through a few oddly shaped bottles and removed the necessary bandages, unguents, and medicines.

Meanwhile, Oliver was kneeling over the badly shaken young lady who appeared to be only a few years older than he. Despite the straggly hair, dirty face, and disheveled clothing, he noted that she was quite comely.

"What are you doing out here unescorted?" he inquired, since Turner was busily fiddling with dressings and salves. Medicinal odors immediately filled the enclosed space.

"A dreadful mistake, really." Her soft blue eyes focused on him; her phrases became more coherent.

"Slight case of shock." Turner rumbled amidst the clutter on the counter which served as his worktable. Normally strewn with all manner of bizarre oddments like explosives stakes and half-assembled timing mechanisms, the work area was hard put to contain the medical paraphernalia occasioned by the visitation. "She'll pull through in no time."

"It's enough knowing I'm in friendly company," she said in her vibrant contralto. Yes, *that* was the kind of voice Oliver liked in his ears.

Turner had removed her bonnet, and Oliver could see that the lady's hair, a splash of molten gold, complemented the smooth cream of her complexion. But the best was revealed last: as she opened her mouth, Oliver was delighted to discover white, clean, even teeth. Perhaps a complete set.

"I'm feeling immensely improved already. In fact, I hate to bloody the clean covers of this cot . . ." She made to rise, but Oliver gently restrained her.

"Nonsense. You'll not get up until Geoffrey's attended to your wounds."

The young woman did not resist, but settled her head back into the pillow. "That's very gentlemanly of you. Your friend's name is Geoffrey you say? What's yours?"

"Oliver. Oliver Dolan." He indicated the portly man at the counter. "Geoffrey Turner." He turned the finger to her and smiled questioningly.

"And me?" A faint smile flickered into her eyes like a dawn sun through morning fog. "Penelope Reynolds."

Turner had collected odds and ends in his chunky fists, and hauled them to the bedside where he dropped them onto an unoccupied section of the cot. "Happy to meet you, Penelope. You'll have to be still now while I administer these little potions. Then we'll wrap you up a bit."

Penelope nodded.

Stepping back to allow Turner more room, Oliver observed as the big man carefully applied his medicine, his bandages, and his friendliness. By the time he was through, the woman was in decidedly better shape, emotionally and physically. The faint aura of Penelope's sweat—Fernwolders were wont to refer to it as a lady's "glow"—gradually gave way before her delicate lilac fragrance, though *that* barely penetrated the miasma of Turner's remedies. To Oliver it was the scent of summer in a flower-flecked field bordering a brook.

Regarding his handiwork, Turner seemed pleased. "Right. The final touch." He hefted a bottle of what he said was his best liquor from the cabinet, poured a dollop of rich brown liquid into a small snifter and passed it to the woman, who was now sitting against the inside walnut panel of the van. "If there yet remains a twinge of pain or the odd speck of depression from your ordeal, this is sure to cleanse it away." His eyes twinkled and he could not help but pour himself a measure—just to be sociable, of course. He extended the bottle to Oliver, eyebrows raised, but Oliver declined with a small frown. Turner drank entirely too much as far as the young man was concerned.

"Well then," said Turner, "Tell us first what happened, and when. Was it a nightcreature?"

The woman sighed and smoothed back a stray curl of hair, then sipped at the snifter. "Not exactly. My horse Charcoal threw me, and I fell down a long, rocky incline." She pointed vaguely in the direction the van had been headed. "Up the road a bit." She took a long pull at the liquor. "I was traveling toward . . . Golly, that brew of yours stings!" Penelope paused to wipe the tears streaming down her cheeks.

"Peterston?" Oliver prompted, casting a grimace at Turner.

"Yes. Peterston. Anyway, as I was trotting along the road, I heard an odd sound. I thought it might be someone in need, so I turned off the road. A few yards into the brush and up a slight incline I encountered a cave. Curious, I neared its mouth and suddenly growls and snarls arose from it. They frightened me, I can tell you that, but not as much as they did my stallion. Charcoal bucked and threw me. I must have lost consciousness. When I woke, I was at the bottom of a hill, bleeding, and in the ragged condition in which you first saw me. I couldn't find poor Charcoal." A note of dismay entered her voice.

Stroking his beard thoughtfully, Turner nodded. "A cave, you say. Growling. Tell me, Penelope. Was the growling and snarling like that of dogs?" As Turner spoke, the smell of alcohol began to dominate.

"I hardly had time to notice that . . . but now that I think of it, why yes, it was!" She lifted a delicate-fingered hand and touched the cuff of Turner's maroon frock coat.

"What luck!" Turner cried, rubbing his hands together happily. "You've seen a bit of action today, Oliver, and you'll get a chance for some training in this vocation of ours."

"What?"

Geoffrey ignored the boy's bafflement and turned back to Penelope, taking her hand in his and patting it attentively. "There is a community within half a day's ride by horse?"

"Yes," she said. "I just came from there—Ashton. And while I traveled I noticed a small castle atop the brow of a nearby mountain as well. I had not time to stop, but . . ."

"Excellent," chortled Turner, eyes aglow. "We'll have time. And, Penelope, you can pinpoint this cave on the rocky hillside?"

"I'm sure I could," she said, her blue eyes bemused. She crossed her black leather-booted feet and fixed Oliver with a puzzled stare.

Oliver shrugged.

Turner was oblivious to this exchange.

"Excellent! Marvelous!" Wearing a huge smile, he turned to Oliver, clapping his open palms dramatically. "Lad, prepare yourself." He dropped a hand on the young man's shoulder. "You and I are about to venture into a den of monsters!"

They stood at the top of the long, rocky hill. Through a break in some spruce trees, they could glimpse the van, parked to the side of the road, where Penelope was resting comfortably. Before them yawned the maw of the cave. Light probed a scant few feet into it: the rest was black. From the cavity, a foul smell emanated like breath from a corpse's mouth.

Turner nodded. "It's a big one, all right." He adjusted the large canister battery strapped on his shoulders, and patted Oliver's smaller version. "That comfortable on you, lad?"

"I suppose so," said Oliver, shifting his hold on the double-pronged rod that earlier had killed the werewolf, saving his life. "But I can't say I feel too comfortable descending into the midst of sleeping nightcreatures. Are you positive it's necessary?"

Frowning, the bearded man reached into the large bag which dangled from his shoulder. "No. I suppose I'm not. But there is a definite purpose. For one thing, I don't care to pass the chance up." He turned to face Oliver. The cool fall breeze which moved from the valley fluttered his curly locks of black hair, assisting the serious cast his features had assumed. "It's not often I get a chance to raid a den—hades, we call them. Not often that we stumble on them. To wipe out a score or more of these loathsome beasts in one fell swoop—well, that's every HOPE member's dream, I assure you." His words reflected a vibrant enthusiasm.

"What—do you keep score? Does the winner get a prize at the end of the year?"

Oliver placed his hand skeptically on his waist, eyeing the fetid darkness with a contemptuous bravado he hoped would hide his trepidation.

Turner ignored Oliver's sarcasm. "I want to give you some practical instruction in the disposal of these things. You may need such for what we face in the future. There's no better way to teach you than to raid a hades. You must realize, lad—the creatures, save one, should all be asleep."

"But they can *wake up!*" His voice cracked, betraying his true sentiments.

"Not likely. You'll remember that theirs is not a natural sleep, Oliver."

"And they all spend the day in caves like these?" He could not even bring himself to look at the thing now, letting a gesture suffice.

Turner shook his head, patiently. "Not all. No vam-

pires here, for example. They sleep in the ruins of Empire mansions. But the nightcreatures that Satan
modeled on Greek mythology, they are assigned to
dens like these, for sure."

"And what sort of creatures *are* these?" Oliver asked.
His active imagination had already quite unnerved him.

"Come," Turner said, extracting from his shoulder-
bag three round parcels wrapped in paper. "I'll introduce you to the first—the one that guards the cavern,
the one that frightened Penelope's horse. Hold these
for a moment, will you?"

Oliver grabbed the objects with his free hand, while
Turner made a final check of his equipment. Within
the crinkly papers Oliver felt something soft and
squishy. A sweet, familiar odor clung to them.

Finished, Turner hooked an arm around his electrostaff, freeing both hands. "I'll take one of those right
now." Plucking one of the balls from Oliver's hand,
the fat man unwrapped the paper. Inside was a gooey
mass that smelled to Oliver much like—yes, it *was* . . .

"Honey," Turner affirmed. "A cake soaked in honey,
actually. Now hold the others out, ready. I'll need them
both in rapid succession." He waddled toward the cave
mouth.

A faint hissing snarl issued from the darkness. It
quickly slid into a deep guttural growl. The growl was
joined by another—and another. And then the furious
barking began. Paws scrabbled against packed dirt. A
vague figure poised just beyond the light wedged into
the cave's darkness.

"Cerberus!" Turner breathed respectfully. "A cerberus, and it looks like a mean blighter." He picked the
gooey cake from the paper, and carefully lobbed it.
"Quickly now, lad. The others!"

Breathlessly, Oliver handed him another. Turner
quickly unwrapped the honey-sopped cake and hurled
it into the cave. Meanwhile, Oliver tore the paper from
the last, and cast it toward the barking.

Which ceased.

Turner said, "It's working!" in an expectant whisper.

From the cave came sounds of mouths chewing noisily. Lapping. Licking. The smacking of jowls. Clicking, munching teeth. Long teeth, no doubt.

"Right," Turner said, fidgeting nervously. "Get your electric torch ready." Turner drew his barbed staff and pointed it, preparing assault. "That's right," he muttered. "Chomp it all down."

Attention fixed upon the muted clamor of the beast's repast, Oliver dug a hand into his sack and removed the flashlight. Something felt peculiar. He gazed down, and removed the plastic and metal cylinder from his hand, whispering, "Eeukk!" Strands of fragrant goo stretched from hand to electric torch; a gob of honey had attached to his palm.

Abruptly, an explosion of howls and whines erupted from the darkness, and Oliver's eyes jumped from the mess to the cave.

"Now, Oliver!" boomed the fat man.

Stumbling forward awkwardly, Oliver managed to flick on the light. Despite the sticky covering, it pierced through the darkness and fixed upon an astonishing sight:

A dog, the biggest Oliver had ever seen. It stood at least four feet high on all fours, in length it reached a goodly five feet.

It had three heads.

Light reflected three pairs of pain-filled eyes, and three sets of jaws snapped furiously. Blood and black noxious ooze leaked down the short chins and the long, sleek throats, glistening.

The cerberus collapsed onto its side, writhed, and whined desperately, clawing at the empty air and the dark musty, offal-strewn dirt.

"Keep the light trained on the beast!" Turner ordered, cautiously nearing the agonized creature. "I need to spear it properly, or we'll have some problems!"

For a few seconds, Turner feinted at the three-headed dog with his staff, seeking the proper path of attack.

And found it.

Belying his girth, Turner lanced forward with surprising speed, puncturing the dog precisely in its oil-dark chest. He buried the twin prongs as deeply as possible into the flesh and metal. In pain, the dog wriggled away, obviously weakening. The barks died into whines, the growls into whimpers.

Steadying himself, his face impassive with concentration, Turner clicked on the battery, flowing the current across the electrodes. A crackling: the scent of singed flesh, of burning insulation. The dog's body grew stiff, the heads became limp.

The beast was dead.

Turner's meaty face gleamed with sweat in the flashlight beam as he turned to Oliver. "Easier than I thought it would be."

"What was in the honey cakes?"

"Vials of acid. Greek myths held that to mollify Cerberus, the three-headed dog who guarded the entrance to the underworld, the newly dead would carry cakes soaked in honey, which the devil-dog dearly loved. As you can see, Satan is fairly accurate in programming these creatures for appetite."

Mutely, Oliver nodded.

The big man retracted the barbs of his spear, pulled the weapon from the dead beast, and pointed into the darkness. "Shall we continue then?" He smiled grimly. His soft brown hair was mussed from his exertion.

Reluctantly, Oliver padded warily forward, holding his pronged spear before him, playing the torch beam about a ceiling which dripped with stalactites and cold, wet silence. He wiped his honey-coated hand on his pants leg, muttering disgustedly—but the gunk clung stubbornly.

The chill dampness of the place seemed to attach to the base of his backbone, slide up, and coat his spine with a thin rind of ice. He shivered. This was a nightmare, but it was no dream.

All the dark tales told in his infancy, all the frights whispered among his playmates, had coalesced into reality. He wanted to throw down his weapons and hurl himself from this madness back to the sane world of his home, the safe, comfortable life protected by castle walls.

A chubby hand alighted on his shoulder, a squeeze of reassurance. He sighed away his shivers, inhaled deeply of the dank-tainted cavern air, and advanced.

A few yards farther, the tunnel twisted left. And, shortly, again, this time right. They negotiated the turn carefully, Oliver flicking the beam to cover every possible place of concealment. But of course they were *asleep,* he told himself. Of course . . .

At the end of the turn, murky light seeped out of the near distance. Cautiously, they crept to its source, a shaft descending to the heart of the hill. They knelt and peered into the glimmering depths. Vague stirrings and creakings drifted upward. Sounds of things *moving?* Oliver's heart quickened with relief. Surely Turner would turn back. Besides, the shaft seemed bottomless. To attempt descent would surely be madness!

A hand curled around the electric torch. Turner's hand. The bright beam was directed to a point just opposite on the circumference: the beginning of a slanting trail of not more than six-inches width which inclined curling about the cylindrical shaft. The way down.

Oliver stared at Turner, almost pleadingly. Turner misinterpreted the look. "Very well," he whispered, not so much out of caution or apprehension, but because whispers seemed appropriate to the encompassing mood. "I'll go down first. Watch carefully."

Without further ado, he moved his bulk to the cavern wall and sidled along the lip of the shaft to the dubious path.

If Oliver had been so disposed, he would have taken more note of the nimbleness and the dexterity of the fat man as he placed his feet on the trail, found handholds, then tucked his supplies and weapons carefully away with one hand, lest they fall. But he was preoccupied watching the manner in which Turner negotiated the twisting climb downward—it would aid his own descent, he thought.

But how far down *was* it?

Fortunately, the electric flashlight was unnecessary. The light penetrating from below was sufficient.

Sounds below echoed hollowly. The cool underground air was laced with nightcreature stench and Oliver's stomach was queasy with fear and revulsion. His mouth tasted bitter; the back of his throat seemed as sticky as his right hand, making swallowing difficult.

As Turner descended, he seemed to gain confidence. He stopped, addressed Oliver:

"Not so bad. Begin to follow me now."

Whispering assent, Oliver followed the man's footsteps as precisely as he could. Around the side of the opening. Halt. Secure equipment. Grip the outcropping of rock. Lower left foot, then right, onto the narrow ribbon of ledge.

The descent was tricky. There were patches of slick wetness here and there on the handholds and on the ledge itself. As they lowered, the illumination from below strengthened. The farther he descended, the better Oliver felt. The light revealed the shaft was *not* as deep as he feared. Forty feet perhaps; fifty at most. It was painstaking work, but the farther down they wound, the less vertigo clouded his thinking. As acrophobia ebbed, however, dread of what might await in the chamber redoubled.

Oliver tried to concentrate on the descent, but was only partly successful; his imagination concocted dreadful futures for them both.

Suddenly Turner grunted. The clop of the man's shoes echoed to Oliver that Turner had reached the bottom.

A minute later, Oliver tumbled at his side. Scrambling up, he saw what had kept the man silent.

If halls were sometimes called cavernous, then this cavern could be called hallish. Obviously the nest had been forged from the living rock by machine, not nature. Electric lights shimmered torchlike along smooth metallic walls. Approximately rectangular, the room stretched about a double dozen yards. Every several meters, tall rock columns connected floor and roof. The atmosphere was strong with foul smells: grease, ozone, sweat, spoor.

All was bathed in a ruddy, rusty incandescence which spewed from rocky stands near each column. Slumped beside each pulsing knobby mound was a nightcreature.

Oliver gasped at the number; all asleep, most connected by thick black cables to the charging mounds. At least forty—if not more.

And an incredible *variety:* werewolves, some larger than the beast which had attacked Oliver that fateful night days before; harpies, wings wrapped about their slender female frames, eyes shut in electronic slumber; chimeras; centaurs; demons; cyclopes.

Absently, Turner gripped Oliver's arm and squeezed. "It would take us *hours* to destroy all of these creatures."

"You're right," Oliver said, finding it hard to form the words. "Let's—let's go back."

"Unless . . ." Turner mumbled, thoughtfully putting a pudgy finger to pursed lips. "Yes. That is a *distinct* possibility."

"What?" Oliver wondered, almost afraid to ask. In his youth, whenever he had felt cowardly, he later felt shame. But now he felt none of that at *all*. Any moment, one of the creature's eyes might open. A glimpse of the strangers, and it would alert the others. What hope would there be of contending with this lot all at once?

None whatsoever.

"Power. That's the key, Oliver," the fat man exclaimed triumphantly, eyes darting, searching. "There's got to be . . . yes, *there* it is!"

Gathering his staff closer in his arms, he carefully stepped over the horns, hooves, and sword-sharp tail of a prone demon that smelled like a rotting skunk. Leaning against an upthrust mound, Turner swiveled his head about to Oliver. "I do need your help, lad. That's what you're along for."

Oliver tried to control his trembling.

"Believe me," Turner said compassionately, "I'm just

as frightened as you. One never loses one's fright in this grim business. You just live with it."

Nodding, Oliver lifted his foot, and stepped over the recharging demon.

Dodging and weaving, like an overweight ballet dancer tiptoeing an invisible tightrope only he seemed to see, Turner led him through the immobile beasts to the far side of the chamber where, imbedded in the wall, was a large dark gray block studded with blinking crimson, blue, and white lights.

"Don't know where the power source is," Turner muttered. "But this is the transformer. Not unlike one we've got back at HOPE castle, from the looks of it. And if I'm not mistaken . . ." His thick fingers crept along a bolted panel on the murmuring machine, felt here, probed there. "Good. I think I can open it."

From his shoulder bag, he took a large battered screwdriver, licked his lips, and proceeded to probe a metal orifice with the steel length of the tool. Scrapes and clicks were at first the only reward for his effort. Turner frowned, twisted the tool slightly more to the left. There was a distinct ping, like a muted bell. Oliver started at its loudness, and swept his eyes back to the sleeping nightcreatures. Several stirred; none woke.

"That's where the lever was," Turner muttered to himself, withdrawing the screwdriver. He swung back a metal panel on squealing hinges, and revealed the inner workings of the power supply: wires, transistors, resistors, a block of microcircuits. "Well, I'll be damned," he whispered.

"What?" Oliver craned his neck for a better view. All he could discern were colored wires and oddly shaped metal blobs vaguely lit by a pulsing glow.

"Look where that light is coming from, down deep within its bowels." Turner pointed.

Oliver's eyes adjusted to the darker interior, followed the pulsing light to its source, and came to rest on what seemed a round, many-faceted crystal. Copper and silver wires were attached to the stone with a coppery-gold solder. The stone's slow throb emerged from its very interior. As he watched, Oliver could feel the warmth of its radiation on his face.

"From another world, Oliver. That hunk of rock is a Liefian crystal, a Power Cell Gem. What planet they came from and how they are formed are open to conjecture. Among my comrades, the most popular story concerning them—yes, we have a couple—is that the gems were a natural product of mineral-based alien creatures which stored life-sustaining energy from the local sun in them. The Empire found their planet, farmed the beasts, and harvested them for the crystals, which were then used to power portable machinery. They are rechargeable—simply place them for a few days in sunlight. *And* they are dangerous. They must be handled with care."

"Why is that?" Oliver asked, absorbed in the hypnotic display corruscating in the gem's core.

"Evidently the process that occurs in these crystals is a conversion of, first, energy from sunlight into very dense, very small bits of matter within the crystal, and then reconversion of that matter into energy for the beast—or this machine. The crystals are not delicate, but they are by no means tough, either. To break one open would mean unbalancing the very precise processes, and converting the special matter nodules within into energy—all at once. Result: intense explosion." He turned to Oliver smiling grimly. "Which is just what we're going to do to this one. That should bring this cavern down around the nightcreatures' heads!" he continued with a note of smug satisfaction. The concept rapidly sank in, breaking Oliver's concentration upon the bizarre light patterns.

"But what about *us?*"

"I am considering that. Obviously, what we need is a small explosion to detonate the large one. And that explosion must be timed so that you and I have time sufficient to get *out* of here."

"Obviously," Oliver whispered, regarding the slumbering nightcreatures nervously. "You have explosives?"

"Yes. But no fuse that will allow us to depart with

our lives." Turner's round hirsute face was lit weirdly by the power gem's glow.

Oliver checked his wristwatch. "How much time do you think we'd need?" He sincerely hoped they would just *leave* this place; the stench alone was getting too much for him.

Turner bit his lip, thinking, and looked down at the watch when his dark eyes lit up. "Hold a moment! Here, let me have a closer look at that watch, Oliver."

Puzzled, Oliver unstrapped it, and handed it over. Turner examined it carefully, nodded his head, popped open its glass face, and felt the hands.

"Lad," he said solemnly. "Do you mind sacrificing your watch to this venture?"

Oliver's first inclination was to refuse: his dead mother had given the time piece to him; it was one of the few things he had to remember her by. But he immediately dismissed the notion. "If it will get us out of here alive, no, of course not." He was rapidly learning the importance of practicality.

"Very good." Turner gripped the youth's shoulder emphatically. "You see, Oliver, what we need is some way to delay the discharge of the explosive. I've got a stick of tightly packed explosive, but the fuse is too short. It would blow even before we reached the shaft. There may be another exit—in fact, I'm sure there is by the size of some of these creatures. But it's probably sealed in daytime. No, we need at least fifteen minutes to depart this place, and maybe another five to reach the van and speed away from any stray boulders that may come crashing down the hillside." Turner tugged nervously at his straggly, mouse-brown mustache.

"You think it will be that bad—the explosion, I mean?"

His eyes drawn again to the crystal's heart, Oliver now saw the dazzles as microscopic versions of catastrophic explosions filled with sulfurous smoke and fiery death.

"Yes, I honestly think that it may well blow the crown off this hill. A *lot* of energy is stored in each such crystal. My plan is simply this—we spear the stick of explosive with the electrostaff. I gut the battery canister of all but the most essential wiring. I turn it on—but with a necessary wire disconnected. One end of that wire I'll connect to the short hand of your wristwatch. The other wire I'll place at a point on the watch dial twenty minutes from the minute hand. When the minute hand touches that wire, the circuit will complete itself—electricity will flow through the charge, detonating it."

"Causing the crystal to blow—but only after we've had time to make our escape!"

"Precisely. How does that sound to you, Oliver? It's a little risky, I confess. We could just forget it, turn tail, and run."

Oliver scanned the chamber. Perhaps they would have time here to kill one, perhaps two nightcreatures with the electrostaff. But that might awaken the others. No, Turner was right. Besides, one or two creatures dead: terribly insignificant. And to take the alternative, running away?

He glanced over the creatures, over their bizarre ugliness, breathing and tasting the malodor of their existence, thought about the terror they had each individually caused, and considered the horrors each would wreak if left to pursue its business.

Oliver swept back a clump of his tawny hair and sighed with resignation. "Let's blow the bleeders to kingdom come."

Smiling, Turner chuckled softly. "Marvelous. I was wondering if I had taken proper stock of you back in your homeland, lad. I see I did. So. We must be about our rather detailed work. Step over here. You hold the torch aloft so its beam falls on my work. I must see exactly what I'm doing."

Nodding, Oliver retrieved his flashlight from his bag and, disregarding the stickiness, flicked it on.

Sweaty minutes later Turner carefully touched the cut wire to the watch dial, then made sure that all the connections were properly attached: the dynamite was placed as close to the crystal as possible; the staff was placed firmly; the canister positioned so that it would not prematurely touch the deadly wire to the minute-hand.

"Okay, Oliver," the fat man said, wiping perspiration from his brow with his coat sleeve as he rose. "We have twenty minutes before this hell hole becomes literally that. I suggest we utilize every second."

So saying, he nimbly picked his way over the som-nolent beasts, heaps of horns, talons, claws and teeth clacking amidst chitonous armor and hard, thorny flesh. The feel of electricity was in the air; Oliver felt the hairs on his nape prickle; his skin goosebumped as he trod closely after Turner, whose fatherly presence gave him a vague sense of security.

If anything, the short trek back to the shaft was more difficult than the journey to the energy machine. They moved faster, and with more fear, tilting precariously here, almost kicking a nightcreature there. But at last they began the ascent. Slipping and sliding at times, they negotiated it safely, and with more speed than they had descended. Yet it seemed an eternity to Oliver. Perhaps they had misjudged the time it would take . . .

Turner hefted his bulk over the lip of the shaft mouth, rolled to proper footing and helped Oliver clamber off the winding shelf.

"Not more than seven minutes used in the departure from the den, I think," he said, allowing himself a sigh of relief. "No time to waste though. Let's be off."

Puffing with exertion, Turner bounded around the first of the tunnel's long curves.

Rising to his feet, Oliver lurched after him, but froze in midstride, when he heard Geoffrey Turner's bellow-ing scream echo violently in the cavern.

SEVEN

THOUGH it seemed shock had frozen him for ages, at most it could have been a second. Almost without thought, Oliver unslung his electrostaff and brandished it.

He inched forward over the glistening gravel that covered the cavern's floor. As he did, the scream died. Oliver fervently prayed that Geoffrey Turner had not died with it.

Staff in right hand, electric torch battling the darkness in left, he hastened around the curve.

The light fell upon a chilling sight that brought fear's bitter bile to Oliver's mouth. Startled, he jerked the electric torch, focusing the light full upon the thing, pinning its bright green, monstrous form against the cavern's moisture-slick gray wall. The thing had the scaly body of a large lizard, a long tapered tail, and four sets of gleaming claws that slashed the ground beneath. From the thick base of its shoulders sprouted seven necks, each writhing languidly, each with a separate reptilian head.

A hydra.

The name rang dimly in Oliver's memory. Hydra, the mythical seven-headed serpent. But the scaled green reality before him seemed of much more moment than any mere myth.

The beam from Oliver's torch was returned by fourteen serpentine eyes, green like polished agate, as they turned to him coldly. The fanged mouths opened, hissing with discomfort. The creature made a tentative move forward, yet plainly it was blinded and confused by the bright light.

Well that he had distracted it! Between the monster's front paws lay Geoffrey Turner, apparently unconscious.

The hydra advanced again, clawing the air as though to crush the light. Its musty serpent stench gusted into Oliver's face.

Keeping the light in its eyes, Oliver advanced, gripping the electrostaff tightly.

For purposes of protection, he pulled the battery canister around from his back to shield his chest, as Geoffrey Turner had worn it when he dispatched the werewolf.

He stepped closer, seeking the right spot to plunge the prongs of the staff. Where had Turner said? Just a few inches below the neck—yes. But this thing had *seven* necks!

Also, approach was difficult, what with the tangle of swaying heads, themselves in search of attack paths.

He *had* to do it. And very rapidly. If this creature barred their passage for much longer, Turner and Oliver would be in the tunnel when the energy crystal detonated.

Then he saw his opening. Two necks had tossed themselves backwards, leaving a portion of the neck base undefended. Realizing immediately that there would be no time to dart forward himself, Oliver raised the staff, and hurled it. The staff streaked forward, its sharp points thumped into flesh—and something else. Plastic? Whatever it was, there was the distinct sound of something hard being punctured. Thinking himself lucky to have selected a spot with such thin internal armor, Oliver reached for the battery switch.

A hydra head darted from the left, knocking the electric torch from his grip. The beast moved forward, mouth agape, and chomped on what it surely thought was Oliver, but was merely the canister. A sharp fang sheared a strap and the head gripped the canister's top, ripped it from Oliver's chest.

Stunned, the lad floundered back, smacking the cavern floor and striking the metal flashlight, which skittered farther away, bouncing a crazy zigzag illumination on the scene.

Finding the canister too hard to devour, the head dropped it to the stone floor. The sibilant hissing increased: the serpent thing hurt. A jagged-toothed head worried the imbedded, bloody spear—but its barbs clung tenaciously.

Oliver scrabbled to a crouch, eyes wide in the light-streaked dark. The wire still connected spear to canister. There was yet hope!

Drawing his pistol from his bag, he aimed at the beast's body and fired.

The flash lit the area briefly, orange-red upon the creature. A spurt of black blood below the left-most neck marked the bullet's entrance. The heads screeched, but they seemed stunned more by the weapon's report than by the gunshot itself. Oliver scrambled for the canister, fumbled at the switch, and flipped it.

Instantly, the hydra's heads simultaneously whipped about, chorusing wails. The monster jerked and a clawed foot attempted to wrest the staff from its chest, but was not jointed properly to accomplish the feat.

However, the battery must have taken a beating for suddenly the red light indicating proper operation flickered, then blinked off.

Fortunately, body stiff, the hydra had just fallen to its side. Only three of its heads still moved.

Turner still sprawled senseless. Oliver crawled to him, picking up the fallen flashlight along the way, and ascertained that Turner was not seriously harmed.

Scratches and tears from the hydra's slashes marred his brown waistcoat and frockcoat; blood trickled from a wound on his forehead. But Turner snored healthy breaths redolent of brandy; he was all right.

Oliver quickly lifted him into a sitting position, and shook him.

Eyes still closed, Turner lifted a chubby hand and bellowed, "Once more into the breach, dear friends, once more. Pluck me from the valley of death. Discretion is the better part of valor!" A hasty slap from Oliver stung the man awake. Turner blinked hazed eyes. "Oh God!" he murmured grittily.. "Snakes! Claws! Shouldn't have—"

"No time to talk now," Oliver said tersely, pulling Turner awkwardly to his feet. "Only a matter of a few minutes until—"

"Yes, yes. Of course. I'll be as much help as I can— but I'm so . . . dizzy." Oliver's light fell upon the downed hydra whose three live heads still waved like seaweed at flood tide. "My Lord—we'll never get past it. How? . . ."

"It's about dead. We'll just have to duck the heads. I'm not even sure it's aware of us now," Oliver remarked, urging Turner's fat form forward. "We'll just have to take the chance, and do it quickly."

"How long have I been out?" Turner asked, shambling ahead as best he could.

"Too long."

They pressed themselves against the damp, slick wall opposite the dying hydra, squeezing away from the length of the thing. Had he so desired, Oliver could have reached out and touched its burned hide. The undulating heads twice came close to striking them, but seemed too preoccupied with their own pain to pay heed to the two men.

Once past the beast, Turner and Oliver increased their speed. But Turner's pace was hampered by the fuzziness his head blow caused him. They limped along as best they could.

Turner pushed Oliver away. "Go on, lad. You don't

need this pile of blubber hampering your speed. Get out." He commenced to wobble forward on his own. The youth pretended not to hear, grabbing Turner's arm again. The very thought of abandoning the man was repugnant.

Together they jogged through the cave mouth into the late afternoon, then stumbled down the hill. Midway down the slanting, grassy knoll, Turner tripped, fell heavily, and rolled, wrenching Oliver along.

Head over heels Oliver tumbled down the soft grassy slope, rolling behind Turner. The sky wheeled dizzily above his head. After some moments of this, he had managed to halt himself and to position his feet in front of his body, the ground shook. The tremor knocked him over and he thudded knees first onto the moist sod, spun around in time to see a geyser of flame, dirt, and rock spew from the mouth of the cave. The explosion was shot with intense white light that scarred his vision with red streaks. Midnight-black smoke, veined with crimson flame, bellied from the crater, mushroomed out, covering the sun, shading the hillside in dark shadow.

Instinctively, Oliver dived into the grass, and curled into a fetal ball, arms covering head.

The tremendous blast echoed through the hills, fainter versions of the original sound.

Debris rained down. Feeling the choking dust and dirt pelt him, Oliver braced himself for rocks. None struck. They had run, or fallen, far enough.

When at last the fine, dusty spray ceased, he peeked upslope. A fine haze of dust still tinted the sky a dark gray hue. Above, the peak of the hill was gone, leaving only a smoking, blackened crater.

Breathing a relieved sigh, Oliver staggered to his feet. The side of the hill, once green with luxuriant grass, was now covered with a thin patina of gray, fallen dirt. The taste of the dust was bitter on his tongue. Above, the hill was speckled with fallen rocks. Stones still spilled and rattled down steeper slopes.

Below him, lying in a dirty, tousled pile, was Geoffrey Turner, groaning.

Oliver picked his way down to the man, and shook his dirt-spattered shoulder.

Turner started, reared to his knees, lifting hands defensively. Then he saw it was only Oliver.

"Dear boy," he said, his voice just a ghost of its usual boisterous tenor. He made a feeble attempt to wipe the grit from his face and hair. "Next time I decide to blow up a Liefian crystal, try to talk me out of it, all right?"

"But where did the hydra come from?" Penelope asked as she attended to Turner's cuts and bruises.

"You'd better believe *that* was my predominant thought when I ran smack into the thing," Turner quavered from the cot. His hands still trembled slightly. Gripped in his right fist was the familiar bottle, almost empty of its pungent amber contents.

"There were other branches to the tunnel past the opening of the shaft," Oliver noted, keeping his attention on the road as he drove. The westering sun was lodged between the peaks of two distant mountains. Its bright orange had coppered, casting eerie light on the land. "Must have jumped across the shaft while we mucked about below."

"Thank God it didn't come down," Turner slurred. He upended the bottle, swallowed. Sighed. "So here we are miles from the nearest community, with the sun about to sink from sight. I'm a fool." He belched bleakly.

"But you said that this van has quite adequate protection to spend the night," Oliver countered, swiveling his head with alarm to gaze a moment at the prostrate Turner.

The fat man lifted a relaxed hand in a helpless gesture. "Oh, certainly. It's quite able to withstand attack from your average wandering whatever. But if I know Satan at all, he's going to kick his infernal troops out in force tonight, looking to crush a certain pair of enemies."

Oliver could barely keep his eye on the rutted road.

"But how does he know it was *us?*" Clammy paranoia awakened in the pit of his stomach.

"Oh, he'll know. He'll know. The eyes of the hydra probably transmitted pictures to Hell."

"We'll just have to drive all the way to Ashton, and hope they'll open the gates for us," Oliver said.

"Not necessarily," Penelope said, rising from her gentle ministrations over Turner. "Like I said, just beyond that hill there . . ." A slim, well-shaped arm streaked past his head, pointed. Oliver noticed a bracelet of pure black metal around her arm. "There's a very small fortified castle. Not a community, but I've heard that they welcome visitors if the need is sufficient."

"Oh, the need is sufficient," Turner cried emphatically. "If we want to see another dawn we'd best seek the place out. I should have thought of this before."

"Does he always drink so much?" Penelope asked Oliver, nose wrinkled at the odor of the spirits. Oliver nodded sadly. The woman breathed a sigh, and, after giving Oliver specific directions, returned to finish bandaging the muttering fat man.

The sun was gone.

Even if you've lived with it all your life, Oliver Dolan thought, you never get used to the coming of Nightworld. There was something preternatural and elemental about it. It touched the human mind in places words would not go; there could be no proper description of the tendrils of dread that curled about one's heart as the night's somber shades coated the land.

Stars salted the sky, winking memories of the sunlight. Neither cold, pocked counterfeits of the warm, life-giving sun had yet risen. Even the trees flanking the rough, weed-fringed road seemed to shake with constant fear—but it was only the night winds. The wide silver beam heralding the van stabbed bravely into the night, but the dark rapidly flowed back to fill the vehicle's wake—darkness on Styx was not the absence of light, but something tangible, almost palpable. The popular tendency was to consider light as the absence of the dark.

Watchful for the night-pack Turner had predicted might descend upon the inadequately prepared van, Oliver mused on light and dark, good and evil, and wished for sight of the castle Penelope had promised was ahead.

"What are you thinking about?" The woman's smoky contralto came from behind him.

"I don't know. Finding refuge, I suppose."

"It's close."

"I've not really had the opportunity of talking to you. Just who are you, Penelope? It's not exactly common to find a young woman traveling unaccompanied across the lands of Styx."

She hung back from him, not speaking. He could hear the soft purr of her breath, could smell the faint scents of soap and perfume and something more. But most of all he could sense the presence of a woman.

"I am a traveler," she said finally. "I am touring the land and its communities." Each word seemed measured, weighed, considered.

"But for what reason? Surely there must be *cause* to wander about so."

"Curiosity," she said, noncommittally. "I shall have to leave it at that for now. Perhaps I'll tell you more, later."

That would have to do, then. But if anything, her answer piqued *his* curiosity, made him want to know more about this unusual person. Most of the women of Fernwold were quite transparent to him as far as their intentions and thoughts went—the only mysteries about them were of piddling social matters. But this Penelope, there was the feeling of importance about her.

"You've not had the opportunity to tell me your mission, Oliver," she said, coaxingly.

"I'll trade."

"Unfair bargain," she said, a smile in her voice.

Oliver shrugged. "Oh well. Geoffrey's probably only

too willing to let you know. I might as well have the pleasure of telling you."

And he did.

He told her how he had come to meet the night-creature-killer, of that man's background. His voice choked as he spoke of the coming of Satan's dragon, and the damage wreaked upon his family. He told her of Geoffrey Turner's ultimate quest.

She was quiet for a while after his tale. Thoughtful.

The van slipped slowly through the night, as the road angled into a sharp turn. From the other side, they could see the castle.

A moon was rising. Charon. When first sighted, it perched upon a distance summit, filling the valley below with milky light and outlining a manse on the hillside above them. A small castle by Styxian standards, it had but two towers and a few perfunctory parapets. The high wall, a prerequisite of all settlements on Styx, hugged the stone structure tightly. Pale light gleamed from windows—a reddish hue; much different from the stark white moonlight.

The access road was a short distance away; Oliver turned into it. The wheels crunched on the gravel as the van moved toward the gates.

He halted the van a few yards short of the large wooden doors, slipped into neutral, and applied the hand-brake.

"Now we must persuade them to let us spend the night." He regarded her briefly. Knees drawn up, she was sitting on the floor. A dim bulb back-lit her hair, making it a cool-fire corona of orange and yellow. The shadows that caressed her face and body accentuated her attractiveness. But those lines of her face seemed *designed*, rather than a random collection of parental characteristics. They were that perfect—smooth, symmetrical, aesthetic yet specially accentuated into an idealization of facial structure.

If this young lady came to my gate, thought Oliver, I'd be *more* than inclined to allow her to spend the night.

He stood up from the contoured seat, unlatched the front hatch, and slid it open. "Come on. Let's see if there's anybody home."

The arched Norman doorway stood imposingly before them, ten feet high, eight wide. It was bordered with wood carvings barely distinguishable in the silver swath of light from the van. Pendant to one of its two dun-colored oak wings was a brass knocker, crusted green with corrosion, shaped like a snarling, clutching gryphon. The smell of moss and mold filled the air, damp with a fog that tendriled from the dark valley over which the castle perched. Oliver lifted the cold metal, and dropped it.

An echoey thump boomed, reverberated from the unknown within. Oliver repeated the knock several times, then stopped, warily checking the surroundings for wandering nightcreatures. An electrostaff was tucked under his arm, a pistol in his deep frock coat pocket, just in case.

Penelope stood by him, face obscured by a hooded purple cape. Turner still slumbered in the van. Best not to display him to prospective hosts in his present condition.

The shrouds of evening layered the land. Twinkling stars splashed the sky, partly obscured by shredded sheets of gray and cream clouds. The dark covered all like a cold blanket: nestled in the sparse, rustling skeletons of maple leaves clinging to branches; laced in the mist snailing over the ground blindly, trailing earthy fumes and moist chill. Oliver was sure it was early enough that the knockings would not disturb anyone's sleep. Footsteps pattered beyond the thick, iron-ribbed door. The opening peep-hole creaked. A bloodshot eye glared at them.

"Yes?"

Oliver nodded at Penelope. She pushed her hood off, threw back her lustrous fair hair, and, as Oliver had instructed her, spoke in a helpless tone. "Greetings. We are travelers delayed in our journey to Ashton. We seek only the protection of your walls, and a place to park our vehicle. We shall be of no more trouble than that to you."

The eye squinted. A man's voice squeaked. "Where be ye from?"

"The province of Fernwold," Oliver answered.

"And what be your business *out* of the province of Fernwold?"

"Really, sir," Oliver said, exasperated. "We ask very little. You can rest assured we're quite human. We don't *look* like nightcreatures, do we?"

"A point there, man. A valid point. But the guile of the Evil One is without limit. Lord knows, ye may be creatures of the Devil garbed as men." The man was quiet a moment, considering. "But I think not. I think not. Just a moment. I'll open the doors for ye, and your vehicle."

"Thank you very much, sir!" Oliver piped as the peephole shut.

They reboarded the van. After a few moments, the large doors swung back, and Oliver drove through the opening into a small courtyard.

He turned the engine off, and exited from the front hatchway onto the hazy, dank courtyard lawn.

From the shifting shadows shuffled a gnarled man, holding a hurricane lantern. The gamy odor of an un-washed body wafted before him. "I be Tarleton Briggs, the servant at this estate," he said, deformed arm gesturing to the castle. "A fine establishment, eh? Is the master's home not a *splendid* example of stylish architecture?"

Lit by the rising orb of the moon, it was quite atmospheric. Though not a wide castle, it was a tall one, walled with surprisingly smooth, age-blackened stone. With the frost and sepia shades of the moon and the night leaching any other color from the slate roofs, cracked cupolas, and stained, ivy-veined ramparts of the fortress, it looked like a sculpture of milky ice. Rearing stiffly into the night sky, it seemed so brittle it might fissure and collapse at any moment. It had none of the stony solidity of Oliver's home castle.

"Yes," Oliver said. "Quite nice."

"Indeed, indeed," the twisted man twittered, twitching fingers ringed with gold and rubies. "I have great pleasure boasting of the master's castle." He raised the lantern, let its pale light fall full on them. "And what be your names, strangers?"

"The young lady is Penelope Reynolds."

"Charmed." Tarleton swept off his battered tricornered hat, bowed with a flourish. He turned a smile full of rotted yellow teeth on Penelope, gave her a quivering wink, fetid breaths quickening.

Oliver cleared his voice, gave the servant his own name.

"Yes, and a pleasure it is to meet *your* acquaintance." The little man gripped hold of Oliver's hand, squeezed it damply. A nod of enthusiasm jiggled long, greasy locks free from beneath his sweat-splotched hat.

"And I'm Geoffrey Turner."

Surprised, they turned to the van. Turner, looking a little flousy and tattered, leaned against the van.

Tarleton's scraggly eyebrows shot up. He scowled at Oliver. "You didn't tell me about *him.*"

Oliver smiled awkwardly. "Can you blame me?"

The servant's filthy face split into a crooked smile. "No." He wheezed with laughter. "I suppose not."

Turner waddled over to him, obviously still feeling his liquor, and thrust out his hand. "Much obliged for your hospitality, sir," he proclaimed, weakly.

Tarleton Briggs took the hand, shook it. "And now, if you'll kindly step this way, I'm sure Lord Billington would deem it a rare and unexpected pleasure to meet you." He pivoted, swirling the black tails of his coat, and hopped onto a paved walk. Weaving and shuddering, he scuffled to an open door.

"Have you served Lord Billington long?" Oliver asked as they followed the manservant into a long corridor.

Tarleton shut the wooden windowless door with a clunk. "Long enough to know he enjoys visitors."

Without warning, Tarleton pounced to the floor on all fours and sniffed noisily at the bottom crack between door and frame. He paused, and peered up, scratching the patchy black stubble on his chin with long dirty fingernails. "Ye don't snuff the night vapors still, do ye? Master can't abide the night vapors."

"Uhm," Oliver answered, unable to catch any more than the musty smell of damp wood and the effluvium Tarleton himself exuded. "No. Nothing at all."

"Can't be too careful 'bout them night vapors," Tarleton said, cackling as he stuffed the crack with bit of gritty, foul rag from the deep pocket of his coat. "Lets nasty things in, it does."

"Do others besides yourself and your master reside here?" inquired Turner, staring curiously at the scruffy man.

"Oh, yes. A few," returned the servant who suddenly bounced back to his feet, then spent several perilous seconds fighting to maintain his precarious balance. "This way, please." He showed them down the corridor, through a large chamber decked with ancient black velvet drapes and somber portraits of scowling, hawk-nosed men. "You have arrived too late for supper, but just in time for brandy. M'Lord is in his library. I shall take you there."

As they were led through twisting hallways and up a winding claustrophobic flight of steps, Oliver could not help but interrupt the solemn silence. "Pardon me, Tarleton. But why does Lord Billington choose to live so apart from a community?"

The manservant rocked to a halt at the top of the steps, and twirled. "Ye shall have to ask the master that, won't ye?"

Did he see a smile tremble at the corner of the man's mouth? The servant turned before Oliver could be sure.

Tarleton stopped them before a door and rapped on it lightly, twice. Then he entered, stooping half his body in.

"M'Lord," the words were muffled through the thick walls. "A trio of unusual visitors seeking shelter from the Nightworld. I took the liberty of allowing . . ."

"Excellent. You did quite well, Briggs," a fainter voice, deeper in the room, responded. "Do show them in."

Tarleton shuffled back out, beckoning the party to enter. "As I thought he'd be, the master is pleased." The crooked grin seemed frozen on his features. He teetered slightly from foot to foot, as though nudged by some phantom wind.

Always the gentleman, Oliver allowed Penelope to enter first, then followed. Geoffrey Turner brought up the rear, eyes darting about suspiciously.

They entered a comfortable room where walls were lined with crowded bookshelves of walnut, umber curtains framed windows overlooking the courtyard. The atmosphere was pleasantly touched with the aromas of cologne and tobacco. In the hearth a fire muttered; warm orange light was cast over a cluster of high-backed armchairs grouped nearby. From the shadowed depths of one rose a tall, mustached man wearing a blue and white evening robe over black dinner clothes. An open book was hooked over the side of his chair; a brandy snifter sat on a squat teak table nearby, glittering amber in the fire-glow. The man, who must have been in his late fifties, groped to the side of the chair for something, found it: a cane. With the aid of this silver-headed stick, Lord Billington moved forward a few steps, nodded in a greeting made cheerier by a warm smile and bright eyes.

How different was master from servant, Oliver observed as the crabbed Tarleton shambled tentatively up to his Lord, waiting for further instructions. Curious indeed.

"Well, well," the old man said in a voice brittle but kindly. "Caught midjourney by Nightworld, eh?"

Attempting to assume leadership once more, Turner moved forward, bowed graciously. "We are most grateful for the shelter you provide us."

"Oh, pooh." The old Lord gestured a dismissing hand toward Turner. "A pleasure to have guests. One gets so weary of the same company all these—years." He waved blithely toward his manservant. "Introductions, Briggs, if you please."

Promptly, pointing, Tarleton Briggs identified each visitor.

"Thank you, Briggs. You will bring up suitable refreshments for our guests now."

The manservant nodded and departed.

The old man leaned onto his cane. "A bit loathsome, is poor Briggs, but you'll not find a better servant west of the Balkan provinces. Now, to introduce yours truly—I am Leslie Carruthers, Lord Billington. Myself and my estate are at your service."

He returned to his chair, indicating the other seats. "Do sit down, and make yourselves comfortable. I imagine you've had an unpleasant experience out there. You all look a bit tousled, if I may say so."

The warm welcome was eroding Oliver's caution. As Penelope and Turner settled in the overstuffed chairs, he could see that they, too, were feeling at home. A nice sensation; Oliver savored it as he sat on a plump cushion, which sank gratifyingly, fragrant with the homey scent of old leather.

"Ah! There," proclaimed the Lord. "Now isn't that much better?" He leaned his cane to the side of his chair, picked up a poker near the fireplace, and worried the hearthlogs so that sparks and new warmth radiated. "This fall weather is tricky, you know. You think it warm, then *snap,* it's freezing cold. There. Much better, no?" He sloped back into his chair, regarded his guests contemplatively. "But you've not had time to tell me what brings you trekking across the Nightworld countryside."

Oliver glanced at Turner. Obviously the man was considering the wisdom of informing their host of the truth. Turner noted Oliver's gaze and his nod signaled that he would answer the question.

"To be honest, sir, we can only relate parts of the

reason for our journey," he said, a pudgy hand running gently over the detailed brocade of the chair's arm. "But what we can tell you, we will."

"Oh, that should suffice. I don't mean to pry." The old gentleman's eyes twinkled.

He placed two fingers to a ruddy cheek and smiled congenially, deepening the fine network of wrinkles, faintly tinged with the red of burst capillaries around his prominent nose. His hair had the color and sweep of a black sea wave, frothing white at the wide curve of his mutton-chop whiskers.

"Very well. We're sure you have only the best of intentions." Turner attempted briefly to preen himself but succeeded only in looking rather ridiculous in his disheveled attire. "I am a member of HOPE . . ."

"Ah, the Holy Order for the Preservation of the Empire!"

"You've heard of us, then?"

"Oh, *indeed*. And only good have I heard of your order, at that. In fact, when was it? Yes, last *year* I entertained a gentleman from HOPE. In fact, he had a van much like yours." Touch of finger to thin lips; a smile of remembrance. "Name of Bradley Highsmith. Nice young fellow."

"Right. Bradley. I know him."

"Quite. He told me much of your organization. How you journey about ridding the countryside of Nightworld sorts. Now, I must admit, I've known of HOPE for some time . . . in fact, I know something of your origins, and something of what this world was before the coming of Nightworld to this planet."

"Indeed, sir?" Turner's eyes opened wider, shining with interest.

"Yes, yes." Billington turned and waved a liver-spotted hand toward his shelves. "My books. Oh, I've lots of old books. Books from before Nightworld. Yes, yes, many books."

"Why do you keep them to yourself?" Penelope asked, daintily propped in her chair, erect and poised.

"Why don't you share their knowledge with the other human citizens of Styx?"

"Why, dear girl, nobody *wants* them!" Billington leaned forward, settling the blue-veined hands of his long arms upon the knees of lanky legs. "Tried *that* for a few years in my youth, don't you know, after I discovered them in the attic of this estate, then newly inherited. Any visitor that came by I showed the books, explained what they had to say. But do you think the people believed me? No. They accused me of heretical nonsense. Fact is, I'm excommunicated from the local church, not that I ever *belonged* to the local church, but that indicates the local attitude toward me. Oh, there's knowledge aplenty of this world for people who really seek it . . . but no one cares to. They like the black-and-white world they live in now. Think about it. It's the truth."

"Except we of the Order," Turner reminded with some pride.

"Oh, yes, the Order. Well and good, the Order, but somewhat delusioned all the same." He picked up a bark brown meerschaum pipe from a reading stand and began to tamp stringy tobacco into it from an embossed tan leather pouch.

"On what grounds do you base that assumption, my Lord?" Turner asked, eyeing the pipe enviously.

"What's your purpose, sir?" the old man rejoined quickly, striking a match and touching the flame to the pipe bowl. A bitter-sweet aroma accompanied blue-green smoke scuds.

"Why, to rid this world of Satan and his minions."

"Ah, yes." Lord Billington puffed more smoke then sighed with satisfaction. "But what is the *true* purpose of the Order?"

"What do you mean?" Oliver asked, wanting to join the conversation.

"P.E., my friends," said Lord Billington, settling back relaxedly, and speaking in a smooth baritone trill of self-confidence. "P.E. Preserve the Empire. *That* is the purpose of HOPE. But, good people, exactly what is, or rather, *was* this—uhm—Empire that Mr. Turner's organization seeks to preserve, eh? Have you records describing the Empire, sir?" Billington directed his pipe's stem toward Turner, who twitched his still ratty beard and seemed profoundly upset with the turn of questioning.

"We have a few hints. A book here and there in our archives." He harrumphed and leaned imperiously forward to offer offense: "But whatever that Empire *is* or *was* it's a sight better than our existence now: Styx in the control of a powerful madman with theological delusions on a mass scale."

"Pah!" the tall man cried, brandishing the pipe like a club. "Talk of delusions! How about historical delusions on a *galactic* scale!"

"What do you mean?" Oliver repeated, honestly curious.

"I'm not entirely sure," Lord Billington said, chewing animatedly on the pipe stem. "But from what I've gleaned from these myriad books of mine, the galaxy-wide Empire that once controlled this world and made it what it was, contributed toward what it *is,* was a historical *sham!*"

Turner fidgeted uncomfortably, rubbing his hands together. "Not true," he muttered. "Not true."

"Yes, a historical sham. A counterfeit. A humbug. An imitation of what once was." Billington's eyes widened challengingly.

"False, sir!" cried Turner. "The original Earth Empire upon which the interstellar empire was modeled was but a foreshadow, a prototype of the glory of the intergalactic empire the brave *English* people of Earth built across the stars." The man was red with bluster. Tears glistened in his eyes. "The bravest Empire the stars have ever shone upon! And it had the most glorious Queen!"

"Who still has the most loyal subjects, I see," Billington observed. "Obviously you know more of this Empire than you've told your companions."

Recovering control of himself, Turner leaned back

in his overstuffed chair, folded his arms. "We of HOPE seldom talk of such things. It would seem ridiculous to the masses."

"*What* are you talking about?" Oliver asked. Penelope too seemed interested in the discussion—her blue eyes burned with curiosity.

Lord Billington made a tent of his fingers and placed the manicured forefingers against his bulbous nose, considering. Then he spoke: "We of Styx are but a solid shadow of another planet's past. I take it you are familiar with Earth, Mr. Dolan, Miss Reynolds."

"Yes," Penelope answered, looking to Oliver as though for support. "The original home of mankind."

"Quite. And the original home of history, as well. The century that mankind began industrialized civilization was influenced principally by a breed—race, if you will—of humans called the English, or British, rather."

"English—the name of our language!" Oliver noted, fascinated.

"Yes, these people originated our mother tongue. At any rate, *they* had an Empire that spanned their globe. An Empire based on national pride and purpose. A truly self-righteous Empire, the like of which Earth had never known, ruled by a rather priggish little lady named Victoria."

"Sir, you malign her!" Turner objected.

Billington smiled. "The British Empire—the Victorian Empire, call it what you will, that is what it was. And, like all Empires, it died."

"But what does this early Empire have to do with the empire which colonized Styx?" Oliver asked.

"Much," Billington said. "For you see, by some freak occurrence, for which I've found no explanation, by some quirk, some twist of fate, the originators of the Earth, or, if you will, Terran Empire, decided to model *their* rule of the stars after England's rule of the waves and the lands those waves struck."

Lord Billington raised both hands, fingers spread. "Now don't ask me *how,* or most of all *why* this occurred. All I know are the things which my books tell me: that this galactic empire, which was the parent of the colony planet Styx, mimicked the trappings of the original Victorian Empire to an incredible degree. Dress, codes, language—the lot. Not to mention religion."

At this point, the hall door opened, and Tarleton wheeled a wooden cart into the room. Atop a silver tray, quivered teacups and frosted cakes, several bottles of deep red wine and a pair of decanters. The small cakes smelled delicious.

"Ah. I think something to eat or drink would be in order, don't you?" Lord Billington observed while replenishing his snifter with a draft of reddish-brown brandy.

True to form, Turner selected a whiskey decanter from which he filled a cup. "You've supplied the bare outlines of the truth, sir," Turner said after a slurp of his drink. "You've not given your cause for your obvious bad feeling toward that Empire."

"I've no feelings of any sort toward it. I merely speak from an historical viewpoint. Any contempt I may display I have no real grounds for, my dear man. You needn't be so defensive. I merely find the entire concept rather . . . well, amusing, don't you know. I mean, modeling an interstellar empire after an Earthly one . . . rather absurd, don't you think?" Billington swirled the brandy in his glass.

"No," Turner said. There was a pause while he refilled his cup. "No, I don't think it's foolish at all. You'll admit that there was purpose to the Empire—that it had an obvious goal. It was noble. Can you imagine man without purpose, Lord Billington? *That* is the absurd concept to me, sir, and I know that *I* can do a lot worse than strive for the heights achieved during the reign of Earth's Empire, whatever its model was."

"You must admit, though, Mr. Turner—the Queen mentioned in the books *is* rather ludicrous. I . . ." Suddenly, Lord Billington's eyes streaked to a distant corner of the room, and widened considerably. Oliver twisted his neck to see what the old man was gazing so wide-eyed upon, but could see nothing in the shadowy corner, save for the neat lines of bookshelves bathed in soft milky moon glow from a crack in the furrowed hangings.

A muted, crackling whine swerved his attention again to Lord Billington.

The old man's eyes protruded maniacally, wrinkling fresh facial fissures. Terror and anger flushed his ruddy complexion to a mottled wash of pink. His teeth gritted. His nostrils flared. His hands shook; the brandy snifter smashed to the rug, splashing its contents onto Billington's fur-fringed slippers.

"The rodents!" he said, gutturally. Veins bulged blue in his neck as he twisted to confront Tarleton. "Briggs! I thought the creatures were exterminated!"

"I placed the traps and the poison as you ordered, sir," the manservant replied calmly, as though his master's eruption was as perfectly routine as a request for milk in his tea.

"Obviously you didn't trap or poison *those!*" Billington cried, shaking a finger at the corner opposite. He turned to his company. "Do you *see* them? My bane. Oh, mercy, *look* at the things! Look at the rats, the mice, the hamsters, the gerbils! My God, they're crawling out of the woodwork! Do you see? Do you see?"

Oliver and the others craned their necks. Nothing. Not even a scrabbling cockroach.

Quaking, Lord Billington rose, and grasped his silver-headed cane. "They crawl up from the basement at night to torment me, the filthy vermin! In droves! They mean to gnaw on my poor carcass!"

Aided by his cane, he hastened to the corner with a wobbly, jerky gait. "But I'll smash you before you sink your fangs in me. I'll smash you!" He began to beat the floor mercilessly with the head of his cane, each stroke crushing the invisible rodents.

Oliver glanced at Tarleton, who shrugged his bent shoulders. "The master does have his eccentricities. The spell will pass. It's best to humor him."

Turner was smirking, as though the old man's madness implied a personal victory for himself. Penelope simply regarded the occurrence without expression. Forgotten for the moment, a china cup of steaming tea was held untasted in her dainty hand.

"There," Lord Billington said, doddering weakly back. "Bashed the buggers' brains in. Teach 'em to sniff around me, waiting to dig their furry paws into *my* body. Briggs!"

"Yes sir."

"See that the corner is scrubbed tomorrow, and those dreadful bodies are removed. Blood all over the place. Smells like bat dung." He handed his servant the cane. "And see that this is cleaned and polished." Exhausted, Lord Billington collapsed into his chair and breathed with relief. "You must excuse me. Those things are the blight of my life here. I won't rest until they're all destroyed."

"Dreadful beasties, aren't they?" Turner asked, after another sip.

"Yes, yes. Terrible."

"Now," continued the fat man. "Whatever you think of our former empire, you must condone the basic actions of my organization."

"Oh, assuredly. *Most* assuredly."

"Nightcreatures are much worse than rats," Oliver added.

"So, perhaps you can be of some aid to our quest."

"Ah! A quest it is, then? What are you seeking?"

Turner quickly told him of the fallen spaceship, and what and who they hoped to find within. He asked if the old man had heard aught of such a craft in the nearby lands.

"No. Can't say that I have. Afraid not. Only help I can extend to you is to give you beds for the night."

"That's very kind of you," Turner said, slurring his words slightly, drink obviously taking hold. "But we had planned on staying in our van."

"Nonsense! I won't hear of it," Lord Billington said. "Why spend the night in cramped quarters when I have comfortable beds available for each of you? You'll not deprive an old man of the meager pleasure of seeing that his guests are put up comfortably for a single night, will you?"

There was no arguing with the man. Oliver could see that, so he gave in readily. He felt fatigue weighing heavily upon his bones, tying aching knots in his muscles. Yes, a soft bed would be nice under the circumstances. Even if the old man was a bit ga-ga, and his servant was rather strange, the castle seemed safe enough.

Penelope and Turner agreed as well, obviously as tired as Oliver.

Lord Billington bid them good night, and directed Tarleton to show them to their separate rooms.

"This whole wing is presently unoccupied," the manservant explained as he guided them through a nearby corridor. "The servants, myself included, live downstairs."

Tarleton ushered them into the rooms designated as Turner's and Oliver's first. They decided to accompany the manservant as he showed Penelope her room.

The bedchamber was almost exactly like those assigned to Oliver and Turner. Couched in a comfortable cedar and lavender aroma, the room was fitted with all manner of Victorian furniture and cluttered bric-a-brac. Besides the stately canopied, maroon-covered bed, there were superfluous squat, straight-backed chairs, an over-stuffed beige and brown sofa, a worn but clean oriental rug of many muted colors, and even a love-seat. Odd portraits and landscapes decked the walls; tinted daguerreotypes of stern, smug men and bemused women, framed in gold and silver leaf, seemed to sprout out of the bureau, dresser and teak coffee table like grave markers.

They bid Penelope Reynolds a brief and polite goodnight. As he turned to go, Penelope touched Oliver's sleeve. "It's been an interesting day."

He smiled. "If *this* was an interesting day, I've got

the feeling the remaining days of this journey will be quite fascinating."

Tarleton took them back to Turner's room, which was immediately adjacent to Penelope's.

"Thank you, Tarleton," Turner said. "I believe we can see to ourselves."

The manservant gazed at Oliver with faint disappointment. "You won't be needing me to turn down your sheets?" He twitched his mouth.

"Ah—no, that won't be necessary. I'd like to speak with my friend alone for a moment," said Oliver, thankful to finally be rid of the man.

"Very well, sir." Tarleton bowed. "Good sleep, my friends. Breakfast will be an hour after dawn. A household custom. Until then." And he was gone, shuffling away, wheezing at some private joke.

Oliver turned to his companion, who had plopped onto his bed. Turner had snagged a bottle from the refreshment tray. He clutched it possessively, taking occasional sips.

"You want to talk to me, lad? About what?"

"Yes, I do." Oliver sat down on the side of the bed, pointed at the bottle. "I want to know why you've been endangering our trip so by your constant indulgence in alcohol."

"Ah. You've noticed, then."

Oliver crinkled his nose. "How can I help but notice. Geoffrey—why?"

"Simple, lad. Because I've a tremendous thirst."

Exasperated, Oliver heaved to his feet and paced the floor in front of the bed. "But why can't you halt this drinking until our mission is completed? I can see that the stuff is acting like slow acid on you, eating you away. Drinking is your own personal business normally. But when my life, and more important, the *success* of this quest depends largely on your actions, *your* knowledge, why endanger us by impairing your faculties with intoxicating spirits?"

"Ah, haven't heard such a speech since I met up with a temperance worker," said Turner. But he sat the bottle on the floor, and struggled up, facing Oliver, wearing a serious expression. "But no, you deserve a solid answer, one that I've promised to give you long since."

"What?"

"Don't you remember, lad, when I was asking you to accompany me on this journey? Don't you recall the reasons I gave for needing a fellow like you by my side?"

"Certainly. You said you were getting on in age, and on a mission of this one's importance you needed extra assistance."

"And I mentioned I had a problem, didn't I?"

"Yes," mused Oliver. "Yes—I recall you saying something to that effect."

"Well." Turner reached down and patted the bottle. "Meet my problem, Oliver. My crutch, my weakness, my joy, and failure."

Sitting back down on the bed, Oliver nodded with realization. "Of course. I should have realized. I'm sorry . . ."

"Oh, not your fault, dear boy. You're not to blame that this fat body of mine is alcoholic, that the brain within this skull needs to be pickled daily in drink to survive. It's a hazard of my trade and my mode of life. You live with constant fear every day, and you need some sort of relief. Alcohol has been mine, and I'm paying for my indulgence in its comforts. That's the problem I mentioned, and something that you're going to have to live with. As I do."

He chugged a swallow's worth, pulled the covers of the bed off, and began to strip to his undergarments.

"Now, I suppose I'd better sleep it off. We'll have to be off bright and early tomorrow morn, eh?" He belched, and was soon between the clean sheets, snuggling up to his crisply linened pillow.

"Yes," murmured Oliver, standing, walking to the door. "Yes. I suppose so."

By the time he had closed the door behind him, Geoffrey Turner was snoring loudly.

Satan slept.

Slept immobile, crucified on a plastoid exoskeleton, tube-and-wire-laced face lolling as gentle waves of salt-sour nutrient bath lapped against tender skin, a faint memory of a human body—wrapped up in circuitry and complex life-support systems which kept the jelly-fish human afloat in the currents of life.

Satan dreamed.

Dreamed the pseudodreams he had programmed into the computer, into the section he had designated for his subconscious, into that portion storing his memories of Luciferian history. There were encoded visions of the scintillating splendor of Heaven, the thundering throne of Jehovah, the ranks of apple-cheeked cherubim and incense-sweet seraphim choraling God's praise. And the recollections of rebellion: of the Miltonic fall through sopping clouds, streams of angels tumbling in his wake, down down down, swallowed up by the earth, immersed in the scorching lake of ragged fire and molten brimstone. Enclosed in the heart of the world. In Hell.

Fierce pride pulsed through the memories. Strong hatred for the Divine throbbed through them. Better to rule in Hell than to serve in Heaven. Better an independent entity in tortuous solitude than a lackey to some other Consciousness.

The dreams rang with dark poetry, sang with songs of nobility, of selfhood. Around the sleeping mind swirled sparkling ambitions, prophetic glimpses of Satan, triumphant. With no one's aid. Alone, and triumphant. 'You are evil only because to be otherwise

*would be supplication to the Divine One,' the dreams
assured him. 'Therefore delight in evil, because it belongs to You alone.'*

Yes. The glory screamed majestically within him.

*But lately intrusive visions had wormed into his
dreams.*

*One squirmed through now, dissolving the flights of
majesty through which his slumber had projected him.*

A man.

He was middle-aged, with mutton-chop whiskers. He
wore a cutaway red and blue military uniform sparkling
with medals, hung with gleaming platinum epaulets.
His blue-black, full mustache was finely waxed. His
gray eyes glimmered with pride.

The man stood in a precisely cubic, metal room,
before a large rectangular screen imbedded in a wall.
Beside him was a small, newly-polished service robot.

Displayed on the screen were the haggard features of
another military man, garbed similarly, smeared slightly
by electronic snow.

"It's crumbling, Nicholas," the man said wearily, his
face creased and wrinkled, his eyes bloodshot from
lack of sleep. "They've not been able to save her. The
sabotage was too extensive. Mutineers have taken many
of the planets. By the time you receive this transmission,
it will all be over. Styx is being abandoned. We're withdrawing our forces to New London, and Terra, to make
a stand. Whether we'll be successful in preventing a
total takeover remains to be seen, but we must abandon
all contact with extraneous colonies like Styx.

"I have no choice but to leave control of Styx to
you, Wells, and the council of dukes," the glum-look-
ing man continued. "We've not seen eye to eye often.
I'm still not entirely sure your session on Bedlam cured
you. But I've no choice. I must leave Styx basically
under your command. The castles, the communication
network, the computer control center—all highlights of
our Queen's glorious reign, and one of the Empire's
greatest accomplishments. It will be your responsibility

to maintain the human accomplishments and the memory of the Empire as long as you can, keep the Christian faith among your subjects, and carry the torch of British civilization through the long galactic night that may well fall upon us. May God be your guide, Nicholas."

The transmission ended, the screen flickered to black.

The man smiled, and turned to the little robot. "I want all doors to the computer systems sealed from outside access. Change the locking sequence. It's all mine now—I'll not share it. Do you hear that, small one? All mine!"

The man walked to a shiny control console. His image bounced back to him.

Satan remembered that image. It had once been his. Nonsense!

That single word echoed clamorously through the awareness banks, through every cell of his limp body. Nonsense. A figment of imagination. Untrue.

He thought he had wiped out all these illusory memories long before.

Unbidden, another false memory swam into his mind.

"It is simple," he said to a number of strangely shaped androids. *Yes, they were his demons. But what was he doing mobile, walking about in a totally flesh and blood body?* "I have prepared the tank and the mechanisms already. I had to blast open that section of the computer. Access has always been sealed. But who's to stop me now, eh?"

The demons gibbered, waved their surgical tools over their heads, with pure delight showing in their twisted aspects.

"All is in readiness. The banks have been loaded with instructions and your nimble fingers must only follow them. You will graft my body directly into the Computer. And I shall survive for centuries—millennia, perhaps. I shall rule this world for eras yet to come.

What identities shall I assume, little ones? What masks might I wear? Julius Caesar? Attila the Hun? Genghis Khan? Mao Tse-tung? Or shall I be the new Victoria, mock-queen of this backwater planet, eh? Or perhaps Satan himself. You would like that, wouldn't you? Shall I follow through on the whim that caused me to create you creatures? Hmmm?" The demons capered and clapped. "Silence!" the man demanded suddenly. "Enough. The operation will be a long, detailed one. Save your energy for that. Prepare me for anesthesia."

The image wavered as Satan forced himself from sleep. He speared a mental command to the control plexus of the computer: search for and destroy those mental images. But he had done that before—to no avail.

He awoke totally, to a sense of loss.

A part of him seemed chopped away. With what musculature still functioned, he moved to look down at his wilted travesty of a human body: nothing gone. Absurd.

But the sense of loss still weighed heavily on his mind.

From the shadows Beelzebub scampered. The furry Chief Demon prostrated himself. "Your Highness, I have waited here these hours for your awakening, mindful of your dislike of the disturbance of your rest."

"What is the trouble?"

"Den One twenty-nine has been destroyed."

"What!" So that was what had caused the sense of loss reverberations from the lack of contact between his banks and that segment of his network. "But how?"

"Intruders jarred the power crystal with a gunpowder explosion, setting off an explosion of—"

"Yes, yes. I can visualize well enough." All those precious nightcreatures—totally destroyed. Obliterated. Almost too much to bear . . .

"Who did it, Beelzebub? Who destroyed my den? Who?"

"Vague pictures were transmitted before detonation of the crystal."

"Yes. Well, where are they?"

"Visual track 18A, your Grace."

Satan turned and directed his mind to the designated track. What he saw made his frail body quake with anger.

"Turner! And the youth! But how? . . ."

"We don't know, sir."

"I want them found without hesitation. I want them . . ."

"Also, your lordship, a transmission from Haven nine one one awaits your pleasure."

"I can't bother myself with such comparatively small . . . wait a moment. Nine-one-one is . . ."

"Yes, sir. In the same sector as the destroyed den."

"What frequency?"

Beelzebub told him. Satan tuned to it, let the image crystallize in his mind.

The picture wavered, coalesced, then formed the image of an old, tall man.

"Greetings, Lord Billington," Satan said.

EIGHT

■▶■◆■◆■◆■◆■◆■◆■◆■◆■◆■◆■◆■◆■◆■◆■◆■

SLEEP eluded him.

Eyes closed, he tossed, turned, scrunched into various comfortable positions. Oliver searched desperately for the vague key that would unlock the door to unconsciousness. That key dangled tantalizing beyond his reach.

Not that weariness did not bind his muscles thickly, heavily. Not that his tired eyes did not yearn to rest, his mind to wander from reality. A worrisome clump of thoughts stuck in his mind, demanding to be considered, precluding slumber.

Oliver shifted yet again, and opened his eyes. The room was spacious. Moonlight spilled through the windows and the wispy, white curtains that bellied out, pushed by the cool, damp breeze that slipped through the crack between window and sill. Shadows blocked the room solidly, comfortably, as though they were part of the furniture. A thick, timeless silence wrapped everything, broken only by the inexplicable noises old buildings make. Creakings of floorboards perhaps. Squeakings of wind-blown shutters. The sheets and blankets over him were warm and smelled fresh with soap and a trace of mothballs.

Oliver extended himself past the sensory facts of the room. His ears tuned out, away from the noise-spotted silence.

He brooded.

His had been such a placid life before, secure, reliable, steady. He knew who he was, who his parents were, who his God was, and how he related to all. He had a solid, tangible place in his world. His was an important wheel that fit into the machinery of what he knew. Indeed, he was able to look nostalgically at the events of only two weeks ago, before the advent of Turner in his life. The Oliver Dolan who had those experiences seemed tangibly altered from the youth now suffering from insomnia.

Mother dead. Father shown to be, after all, only human. Whole cosmography of creation radically changed—theological assumptions shredded and tossed to the winds. Oliver thought about all this and what it meant to his conception of how things worked.

He had always been a religious person. His prayers had been an important part of his life. His church lessons he had taken most seriously, had enjoyed contemplating. He and his various ministers had enjoyed long hours of discussion on the actual meanings and import of various doctrinal issues in the relationship of God to individual man.

And along had come Turner.

The things the man had taught him did not necessarily prove the lack of God's existence, but the lack of a spiritual Satan—which was a road to the same conclusion.

Considering this, Oliver found himself becoming angry. Had all his beliefs been in *nothing?* Were men, after all—as he had speculated in moments of depression—mere accidents in the Universe: specks of being twinkling a moment in existence, then fading to blackness forever, unmourned?

Was each individual . . . no, take it further . . . was

he alone in the scheme of things? Meaningless against the backdrop of the stars? Purposeless in an unthinking cosmos? After his death, would he simply cease to *be*?

The concept was difficult to accept for someone so attuned to spiritual matters. The thoughts saddened him immeasurably. His very mission with Turner seemed robbed of importance. So what if a madman rules Styx? So what if the nightcreatures overrun the world? What difference does it make in the long run? If *Satan* was a sham, then surely *God* must be a myth.

After all, what signs had God given him of His existence? What fiery handwriting had He put on Oliver's wall? What angels had He sent down to save Oliver from the werewolf? What visions had He bestowed upon Oliver's eyes to refute the lad's doubts?

What had God done to save his mother?

As the realization that his mother was *gone, dead,* never to be seen or heard or loved again, seeped further into his consciousness, Oliver began to despair.

If God did exist, what sort of being was He to *allow* all the pain and insanity that continued in this world? Why, if He did exist, He must be as mad as Satan.

Shorn of the beliefs upon which he had based his life, Oliver began to see life as meaningless. The colors that had enlivened his mind for as long as he could remember, the vivid enthusiasms, his lusts for life and its component parts, began to fade away.

He felt totally alone, understanding nothing and no one. Least of all himself.

Alone in a frightening existence, on a madman's quest with a drunkard.

Alone. Terribly, inexorably, unrelievedly trapped in his selfhood, his oneness.

Alone.

Mercifully, his tense muscles finally unwound, and his fevered mind drifted off.

He awoke.

The moons were gone. The night outside was much darker. Time had passed.

What had awakened him? Tired, he pulled the sheet close to his chin, buried himself in the deep softness of the feather pillows.

A sound pierced the stillness. He sat up. Was that a muffled cry?

Sweeping off the covers, he stepped onto the cold floor, speedily drew on his stiff breeches, his soft shirt, but left his boots where they stood. The lead box Turner had given him was tucked in one of those boots. He considered, then slipped it out and stuck it into a pocket. Turner had, after all, cautioned to keep it by his side at all times.

He tiptoed to the door, silently opened it, peeked out and down the corridor.

Nothing.

A lantern casting a flickering wash of yellow light— that was all.

Perhaps it had been his imagination, after all.

He was about to return to bed, when the door to Geoffrey Turner's room opened. Three figures emerged, edged in the lantern's feeble glimmer, two of them dark, caped, carrying a third, fatter man, obviously bound and gagged: Geoffrey Turner.

Oliver's lungs seemed to freeze. Chill fear flowed freely through him.

As the two figures dragged Turner's form around the corner, Oliver vaguely discerned features in the wavering illumination provided by the lantern. Both had thin, angular features. Both were clean shaven. Through the thin, knife-gash lips of each protruded long sharp canines.

Vampires!

Smooth and graceful despite their burden, they slipped away from sight like dissolving nightmist. Oliver knew he had to follow.

Cautiously, he crept to the twist in the hallway, and peered around it. The two vampires lugging Turner sank down the curling staircase, vengeful ghosts dragging their nemesis into his grave.

After a brief pause to catch a breath of the dusky

air, Oliver slunk slowly to the stairway's peak, and watched as the vampires bumped the fat form down, step by resonating step.

Muted groans and curses began to drift up from Turner. Oliver, careful to keep to the shadows and out of sight, trailed them through corridors, down stairways, to the damp, cobwebby cellars of the castle, where all was floored, walled, and ceilinged in moist black stone. The vampires took the unfortunate Turner, faintly mumbling and grumbling through his gag, into a large dungeon.

Ascertaining that this was indeed their destination, Oliver sidled to the cell, back to frigid stone, listening. Obviously, they had been betrayed. No part of this castle was safe. An escape was necessary, and he had to plan that escape.

"You can remove his gag, now," said a clear, cold bass voice Oliver did not recognize. Then: "Welcome, Mr. Turner. We have long wanted to get you in these circumstances. However We didn't think you'd oblige Us by stepping directly into Our midst. We thank you very much."

"Billington!" Turner bellowed bitterly. "You're in league with these fiends. I've heard of your like, but never thought I'd not recognize—"

"I'm really frightfully sorry, Mr. Turner," whimpered Billington tremulously. "I really and truly am. I . . . I can't help it. I'm as much in their power as you are now."

"Don't complain, Lord Billington. Your efforts on our behalf will be well rewarded, as always. Besides, your drug supply is dwindling, I hear . . . It is well that you've made Satan happy. He will replenish your stock amply now, I think."

Unable to resist a peek, Oliver leaned over, positioned an eye just above the barred window in the stout oaken door. He expected to see a plain room with dirty, noisome beds of straw. That, after all, was what dungeon cells were usually filled with. Instead, he saw a wide, deep, stone-floored room paneled in pale green plastic and gray metal, shiny in cool, steady electric light. Against the walls stood machines, including a red and blue, light-spattered mechanism, centered by a flat black screen, positioned above a number of knobs and dials. Geoffrey Turner was strapped to a steel chair which was bolted to the floor. Hovering were the two vampires, pale sharp faces stolid, eyes like those of dead fish. Another stood closer, outlined by the screen: ramrod-straight, larger, more powerful than the others. The inside of its coal-black cape was crimson silk—the exact shade of the meaty tongue which toyed delicately with a pearlescent left fang. The vampire regarded Turner fiercely. Its head was a gaunt, sallow ovoid set upon the blood-red tray of the cape's flared collar. Its face was death-pale parchment, yet smooth and handsome in a hard disdainful way, bereft of any soft human emotion. Sunk deep in its skull, the eyes glowed with a light that had nothing to do with warmth. It seemed more like the phosphorescence associated with the decay of organic matter in swamps, foxfire that had crawled into the vampire's skull. Obviously the leader. Cringing in the corner was the pitiful figure of Lord Billington.

"We'd dispose of you immediately, Turner," the larger vampire said, voice sinister and precise, "only Satan wishes to chat." He turned, and nodded to one of the underlings. "All right, 493. You can have Billington raise the Master on the communications screen."

The vampire turned, hoisted Billington up. The tall man did things to the controls, his eyes focused ages away.

Enough. Oliver knew he could do little that was effective now. He had to see Penelope, make ready for a clean escape . . .

He would try to rescue Turner then.

Angling back from the door, he quietly retraced his steps up the several levels of the house, toward Penelope's room, clothing himself as much as possible in shadows.

Slinking along a wall, moving with all senses alert,

he heard a movement near the base of the main staircase. He crouched low in the darkness, contained his
breathing.

Ambling awkwardly around the steep side of the bottom stair came Tarleton Briggs. Not noticing Oliver, he
shambled past, obviously headed for the dungeon.
Surely if his master was involved, so was the servant.

Lunging forward, Oliver snared the bent man's neck,
and hurled him to the floor, a hand clamped over the
mouth to prevent an outcry. Oliver had to struggle to
not be sick from the man's gamy stench.

Tarleton squirmed and strained a moment, until
Oliver warned him: "Be still, or I'll still you for good."

The servant stopped moving, save for an occasional
nervous twitch or spastic shudder. Oliver dragged him
the few feet to where pale, yolky light from a distant
hallway lantern puddled on the frayed edge of an ornate rug. He propped the servant against the wall, cau-
tioning him that to make any loud noises would result
in immediate strangulation, then eased his grip.

"Tell me what's happening, Tarleton. It was a trap
all along, wasn't it?"

Muscles tensed in the little man's thin face, knotting
the bloodless lips into a grim, lunatic smile. "We did
not ask ye to come knocking at our door. We did not
lure ye with singing sirens nor brazen invitations. No
one asked ye to set foot within these unfortunate walls."

"But why, man, *why?* How is it that Lord Billington
is in league with these—these dreadful forces?" Oliver
demanded in a harsh whisper. "Why does he give shelter to these fiends?"

"Pah! Do ye think m'Lord's the only human on this
world to aid and abet Satan? You're a fool if you
do . . . and m'Lord does not do it from his free will.
He has this . . . hunger, ye see, which only Satan can
satiate."

"Yes, of course. I heard drugs mentioned."

"Drugs, pah! An understatement for the elixir of
Hell that m'Lord daily receives into his veins. The stuff

sends him to places only to be seen in the mind of man, places he cannot describe."

"And in turn for use of the castle and service to him, Satan provides Lord Billington with these drugs?"

"Yes. That be the situation. We keep a nice little harboring place for the likes of demons and vampires, below. We do a good job for Satan, we do. And tonight we have scored a major victory, trapping you and your fat friend. You won't escape, you know. Do what you like to me, but any way you look at it, you're doomed."

"But Tarleton, I don't understand. Is your devotion to Lord Billington so great that you'll serve Satan just as devotedly?"

The twisted smile contorted into a scowling grin. Tarleton grasped his left shirt sleeve, pulled it over the elbow. The mottled blue-veined stretch of skin above the midjoint was pocked red and pebbled with hypodermic tracks. "Places we go are grand, marvelous, and worth anything to get there," he murmured in a faraway voice. His tongue lolled from his mouth. Fetid greenish mucous and spittle bubbled and dripped onto his splotched tie.

Nothing to do but dispose of the fellow. Oliver struck a blow across the chin. Another. The man flew back, banging his head against the wall, and sprawling in a limp, tangled heap. Oliver yanked the cords from nearby drapes, tied Tarleton Briggs' feet, and stuck the man in a closet, gagged with a strip of his own shirt.

Oliver resumed his journey, hastening to make up lost time. He dispensed with his wariness, in favor of a headlong dash to Penelope's chamber.

Arriving at the door, he pulled it open, dashed in . . . and halted, repulsed, at what he saw.

Lit by dim starglow and the courtyard's meager lamplight mingling with the basic darkness of the room, a caped figure hovered over the bed, beside the prostrate form of Penelope Reynolds. Enrapt in his business over the woman, the man did not seem to notice Oliver's entrance.

The man's sleek, black-haired head was buried against the smooth, white, vulnerable curve of Penelope's neck. Her bodice had been torn half off—partly revealing the gentle slopes of her heaving breasts. The man was bent over her, supported by his hands astride the shivering, half conscious form moaning long and low, imprisoned by unconsciousness and this unhallowed embrace. Obscene sucking sounds rose from the intertwined figures. Stealthily, Oliver stalked round the ruffled bed, dug a hand into the man's shoulders, and wrenched him away.

This succeeded in pulling the man only partially from Penelope—he was like some animate statue.

Eyes gleaming with anger, the intruder swirled to face Oliver. Running down his—no, *its* chin were bright ribbons of liquid red.

Blood.

The vampire snarled, snapped open its mouth with fury, showing fully its sharp bloody fangs. It hissed. With tremendous power, flung its arm out, batting Oliver away, banging him against the wall.

The blow stunned stars into Oliver's vision. He recovered just in time to avoid a clawlike hand endeavoring to crush his neck. He let his feet go limp beneath him, and fell to the floor, rolling away.

But a cold hand encircled his ankle, halting him. Another hand grasped his collar, and he found himself hurtling through the air. He landed badly, the breath puffing from his lungs. Jagged bolts of pain streaked his body. Laying asprawl on the floor, attempting to suck the wind back into his gut, he rolled over to find the vampire, cape billowing eerily behind it, pacing forward.

The thing was incredibly powerful. There was no hope of pitting his comparatively meager strength against it. He wondered if there was *any* hope.

And then he remembered the lead box. He reached

for it, and had the box in his hand, when the vampire grabbed him.

The box fell away to the floor and the hard, merciless hands of the nightcreature quickly dragged him away from it. Those hands hauled him up to his feet, repositioned themselves on his shoulders, holding him there. It felt as though he were being held in a vise.

The thin features snarled up into a hellish aspect. Hellish eyes glittered with bloodlust. Bone-white fangs gleamed as the head bent toward Oliver's neck; metallic breath cold on his exposed skin.

A scream rent the silence.

Oliver, caught up in an almost hypnotic trance from the gaze of the vampiric eyes, was astonished to realize that the cry was not his.

Sharp teeth poised over the jugular, the vampire halted, turned, just in time to catch a blurring foot in the face. The force of the blow jarred the thing away from Oliver, who fell backwards, dazed. The person who had delivered the kick sprang from the door. Penelope. In nightclothes, hair a light flaxen cloud about her head, two red wounds glinting in the faint starlight, she moved past the window toward the vampire.

With motions almost too quick to follow, she pummeled the thing with a dazzling series of blows from the heels of her hands. She chopped at it mercilessly, jabbing, feinting. The still-standing vampire moved back in surprise at the fury of its intended victim's attack. A fist caught it in the nose. There was a crack. Blood dribbled down the thing's face. The vampire snarled with pain, hissed and spit with anger, then swiped at the woman.

Penelope ducked to the right, darting for a swift hold on the vampire, lithe leg snaking forward quickly between its legs to trip it.

A mistake. The beast was too powerful. It grabbed both her arms, and tossed her away as a man might toss a ball. She crashed onto the bed, cracking its ancient walnut rococo-style headboard, which slammed down on her.

The troublesome female dispensed with, the vampire advanced again toward Oliver.

But Oliver had scrabbled backwards. His hands scoured the dark floor for the black box that had fallen from his grasp. He swept both arms over the rough rug, desperately searching for it before the vampire could again carry him away. There was no succor now from Penelope—brave as her onslaught had been, it had provided only brief respite.

His left arm struck something. He grabbed it up with both hands: the hard, cold, heavy box.

He flopped onto his back. Above, outlined against the window, the vampire lurched forward confidently, then floated down to catch him up once more, to suck him dry of his life's blood.

Oliver fumbled with the box's latch. Vampire almost upon him, he tugged it open.

Light seemed to spring into the darkness. The silvery glow bathed the torso of the descending nightcreature in a ghostly glow.

A ghastly grimace replaced the thing's fierce expression. Its cape whispered around desperately as a shield. But whatever force the cross radiated could not be stopped by mere cloth. The vampire staggered backwards, gurgling harshly with anger and pain.

Holding the box between himself and the coruscating cross, Oliver leaped to his feet, and followed the vampire's retreat, hanging in as closely as he dared, but out of reach of any powerful arm swipes.

Peripherally, he saw Penelope recovering.

He angled, driving the thing away from the path that would have brought it to the bed, and provided it with a chance to grab hold of the woman for protection.

He forced the cowering vampire against the window. Already he could tell the radiation was having an effect. The vampire's facial skin was turning blue. Clinking noises, at first vague, but now rising, pounded from its chest. It turned, obviously considering a leap from the window to escape. But they were four floors above the courtyard. However, there was a ledge . . . .

It smashed the window pane. Shards of glass spilled out, scattering down, flashing in the lantern light like a fall of diamonds.

Oliver was about to grasp the spiked cross by the hilt and drive it into the creature's back, when Penelope cried: "Move back, Oliver!"

Caught by surprise, he obeyed. She swung a post from the broken bed toward the vampire, who had one foot already through the smashed window and had just lifted the other. The wood crashed onto its neck, splintered in half. The vampire twisted and desperately clutched for the window frame. It tilted, and toppled with a cry.

The thing tumbled to the ground, and hit head first with a discernible snap.

By the light of nearby lanterns it could be seen that the vampire was dead, its head nearly broken off from its body.

Oliver sighed slowly, painfully, and clapped the lead box closed.

"Damned difficult thing to kill," Penelope commented, while sweeping back her golden hair.

Oliver turned to her. "You all right?"

She felt her neck. "Only a couple of scratches. You caught the thing just in time. I woke up and all I could see were its *eyes* staring at me. Must have hypnotized me, or I would have put up one hell of a fight!"

"You *did* put up one hell of a fight. But there's no time to talk. They've got Turner downstairs. Probably sent that one," he pointed out the window, "to take care of you and me." He turned to tell her to dress, but she was already doing so.

"What are we going to do?" she asked, slipping pants over the nightdress.

"The way you fight, I think I'll just sic *you* on them. I've never seen—"

"I'll teach you some time." She flashed a smile at him as she buttoned her blouse.

"Just remember—we're on the same side. If that

vampire hadn't been partly metal and plastic, there'd be pieces of him lying all over the room."

She slipped on her boots, and Oliver tied a makeshift bandage around her neck.

"All right," Oliver said. *"This* is what we're going to do."

Those visions, those ragged pseudomemories should not have come to him, Satan thought, as he waited the interval between transmissions from Lord Billington's castle. What could have caused them? A frayed resistor? A faulty capacitor? A foul-up in the linkages to the stock of drama videorecordings? Surely they were not part of Satan's actual memories. Surely he had not lived them, for the personage that he associated with himself was obviously a mere human.

There would be time to check. While waiting for Turner to be brought to his attention, Satan would make a thorough scan of his circuits.

He did so.

As always, his mind quested through himself metaphorically. The schematics had turned from mere maps in his mind to components of spiritual essences intricately connected, governed by the will-force located in the life-bath.

Color-coded wires and microchip electronic neurodes, complex technological fruit of a by-gone, more rational age, were not just steel and synthetics to him. Nor was the flesh that held his will merely woman-spawned flesh.

No. This was the present incarnation of the Evil One. Satan. Old Nick. Lucifer. Split-foot. The Devil.

Even his roaming night-servants were parts of him. Minor parts, true, but all formed an intricate network of sight, smell, touch, that focused on the spiritual center: himself.

He warred against the forces of light incarnate in man, viewed the battles, indeed the war itself, through kaleidoscopic prisms of irrationalizations, which fragmented the light of truth into images suitable to his view of reality, murky and dark.

Hence, a given wiring harness was not merely a collection of insulated metal rods distributing electrical impulses to effect results from machinery. No, they were spiritual channels for the life-force flow, veins and arteries of a spiritual being who molded flesh and blood into monsters to serve its will.

Electricity was the distribution of his psychic energy, augmented by other power sources, spiritual all. Energy was the stuff of the Universe; energy and matter. The ebb and flow, the wax and wane between the two constituted the essence of existence, and to be the Lord of both was Satan's ambition. Power was all.

Satan scanned.

No room for impurities. Imperfection must be eradicated.

Reducing part of his consciousness to a small kernel, he flowed through the caverns of the wires, bled his awareness slowly into particular sections of the great computer. To travel each wire, through each circuit, would have taken days, even at the speed of electron transference. Rather, he made a cursory scan first of certain sections, finally funneling into memory-storage neurodes.

He reveled in his more majestic memories as he searched. He bathed himself in his own might and importance, gazed at himself lovingly in the mirror of his memories . . .

Suddenly a current swept his mind into a section of which he had not been aware. And as he hurtled along, he found that these were no neurodes, spiritual nodes to which clung the essences of sight, sound, and reaction which formed memory. No, they were reflections —reflections from a fleshier mind.

He sank, helpless, into them:

Propped in a comfortable antigravity chaise, he was reading a treatise on the influence of Greek myths on medieval demonology when Captain Bartholemew Worthington entered the cabin.

"Styx is on the scope, Colonel Nicholas." The slight

but intense officer was dressed in the powder-blue uniform of the Queen's Imperial Space Navy. "We'll have the *Palmerston* in orbit in just a few minutes." Worthington directed his strong, gray-eyed gaze to the reader screen. "Unusual subject matter, Hedley."

"The pyschs claim it has a sedative effect on the wilder facets of my curious imagination. Fire with fire, you know." Hedley Nicholas stabbed a button to black the screen. He twisted another to cycle off the beige leatherette chair, which settled slowly to the floor. He slid off, rose, and straightened his uniform. "So then. I hadn't expected such a speedy arrival at the planet. It was only yesterday we exited subspace, wasn't it?"

Worthington stroked his dark mustache. "The *Palmerston* is one of the newer models in the Queen's fleet. We can move her with quite some speed if we desire." He smiled a gentlemanly smile and beckoned the Colonel into the corridor.

"And I get a full explanation of why I was suddenly yanked from peaceful recuperation?" Nicholas asked as they marched to the lift station. "Why has the *Palmerston* been selected to whisk me to *this* planet?"

"You were promised such, weren't you?" the Captain said as he touched a button and doors parted. They entered the elevator; the doors hissed shut behind them.

"Not much choice in the matter," the man muttered to himself.

"No, Hedley. Not much choice. The Queen commands. Her pleasure is rule."

Nicholas leaned against the railing of the little liftbox streaking them the length of the starship to the bridge. It really didn't matter much to him. One place was as good as another. The pyschs had okayed it, hadn't they? He could recuperate as well on Styx as anywhere else. Too, there was the work involved. Work could be quite therapeutic. As one of the top, perhaps *the* top, planetscapers in the Empire, he was quite valuable.

And, had he not been so valuable, perhaps they

would have walled him up with the psychobots on Bedlam forever.

A planet to 'scape, then. What else could it be? The question was, what sort of job was it to be? His curiosity was piqued. He was looking forward to his first sightings of the world.

Silence shared the rest of the ride with them, but fled as the doors parted and they stepped onto the bridge.

The screens were full of Styx. The planet hung in space before them, a green and brown jewel on black velvet. "It's beautiful," Nicholas heard himself say.

"Quite a find, eh? Imagine, because of its orbit and its land-sea configuration it enjoys a climate almost matching that of old Britain."

"Ah." A smile touched Nicholas's lips lightly. "The Holy of Holies."

"We have rather modeled our Empire after it," Worthington acknowledged.

"To the chagrin of certain factions."

The captain let that pass. He walked to an instrument panel between a pilot and copilot who were busily supervising orbital insertion, drew a small cassette from the breast pocket of his uniform, and slotted it.

"This little recording was made specifically for you, to be viewed upon near-arrival on Styx," Worthington said, punching 'play'. "Check the video."

Nicholas turned to the hologram tank. A form wavered into focus, solidifying into a middle-aged woman seated upon a wooden throne embossed with rubies and sapphires. A slight, pudgy woman, she wore long, undecorated brown skirts. Her graying hair was tied in a utilitarian bun. At court, the assembled party would have bowed; but this was, after all, only a recording. Nevertheless, Nicholas found the impulse almost overwhelming; he allowed himself a slight nod to the Queen.

She spoke. "Greetings, Colonel Hedley Nicholas. I speak to you light-years and subjective months away, but what I say will be of the same importance when you receive it, as it is now, when I speak it.

"We are not unaware of your unfortunate battle with—shall We say, certain cerebral malfunctions. However, Colonel Nicholas, We are prepared to forego further mention, having learned of your rapid recovery . . . and We are prepared to forgive fully indiscretions committed when you were . . . not yourself.

"In return, We ask only that you give Us your complete attention to the task to which We are assigning you.

"The planet you now orbit is a very special joy to Us and to the inhabitants of Our Empire—it is a very important discovery. We have unique plans concerning it, plans in which you play a vital role.

"The civilized planets that We number Ours are too much with the trappings of modern civilization. Too many are the buildings, insufficient the green and pleasant land. On the planet Styx, We have discovered a world of such landscapes as We desire, a long land and kindly, surrounded by gentle seas which endow it with a climate perfect to Our needs.

"Your task, Colonel, is to apply your planetscaping artistry to the automation of Our planet. Dot it with small communities conforming to the old ways, lacking only the old discomforts. Architecturally, model the world after the medieval heritage of Great Britain.

"Sufficient material, machines, and labor have already embarked for the planet. Further instructions await your planetfall. This is a royal directive to you, requesting your best work, and your loyalty.

"One last word, Colonel Nicholas. Because of your past history, we have selected a trusted member of Our staff to assist you and to ensure that you have no further . . . problems.

"He awaits you on Styx, with the basic workforce, the necessary machinery, and a group of colonists.

"We bid you God speed and good luck. Our desire is that you work toward the basic ideal of the Empire. We ask you to make a paradise, Colonel Nicholas. No less than a Camelot, to last far longer than Arthur's.

The quality We wish, only your considerable talents can achieve.

"Best of luck." She smiled, dimpling her small, dumpling face.

The image faded.

"Well, Hedley," Worthington said. "What do you think?"

Nicholas shrugged. "It sounds like a very nice assignment. But this . . . ah . . . companion of mine . . . is he a? . . ."

Worthington nodded. "Right. A simulacrum. An historical mandroid . . . something Wells. I think I've got a picture of him . . ."

"Your majesty. The transmission is with us again. The communication from Billington Castle . . ."

"Yes. Here it is. Only two-dee. I'll put it up on the screen."

"Your majesty—are you awake? They have Geoffrey Turner on the screen . . ."

Worthington slipped the slide into the mechanism and the picture flashed onto the two-dee screen. A chunky man with a mustache . . .

Satan came to his senses. How . . . What? And that face . . . that face!

That face in his memory, in a fatter, hairier version, gazed defiantly at him from the video channel to Lord Billington's castle.

NINE

※☀☀★☀☀★☀☀☀★☀☀☀★☀☀☀★☀☀★☀☀★

OLIVER Dolan found that the excitement speeding through his veins had chased away his usual fears. Just as well, he realized, for the difficulty of gaining Turner's release was fraught with elements of anxiety.

On the surface it was simple enough. Get Turner out of the dungeon, speed him up to the courtyard where Penelope would be waiting with the van, and then escape through the gate which she would have opened.

But there were the vampires to deal with. He'd had definite problems disposing of just one of them. What would *three* be like?

As Oliver once again crouched beside the door, listening, it was the leader that was speaking. ". . . ages. You've managed to avoid us for a long time. I personally have the honor of being your designated executioner, by the Master Himself."

"Most interesting speaking with him, after all these years." Turner's voice was bluff, blustery, but a tremor of fear was discernible. "Old Satan seemed a bit off kilter, out of whack. Getting on, I'd say. How many years you think he's got left, eh? What's your lot going to do when he withers on his electrical vine and leaves Hell without a master?"

"Impossible," the leader said in a cold monotone. "The Master is immortal."

Turner half-chuckled. "As immortal as I, vampire. Only as immortal as I."

"Regardless of your absurdities, He has what He wishes, a chance to see you below His thumb. I dare say, even now, He is watching the proceedings through our eyes." There was a momentary silence. Then the leader spoke once more. "A shame our host so soon lost his wits to the drug—he might have enjoyed watching what is to become of you."

"Well, maybe you can tell *me*."

"Of course. You may think we're simply going to kill you. Not so. The Master has other uses for your peculiar body."

"What of my companions?"

"Presently satisfying the thirst of a fellow."

A perfect cue. Oliver moved a bit down the dark, echoey hallway, directed his voice further. "Geoffrey! Geoffrey! Where are you?"

"Being taken care of, eh?" Turner said. Laughter was in that voice—but Oliver detected concern as well.

"493. The boy's wandering about. See to him."

Oliver stood behind the door and waited for the vampire to leave the chamber. He had removed the cross from its lead shielding; its warmth . . . and something else . . . tickled his hand.

Leaping, he caught the vampire in midstride, and buried the fiery shaft of the cross-knife deep in the ruffled-lace chest. The creature spasmed, reaching to pull out the knife. Slippery iron-smelling blood streamed red along the hilt, but Oliver kept the shaft buried long enough to do its work. The vampire arched at an impossible angle, then its eyes filmed over. Putrid bile coughed from its tight lips as the thing fell wriggling to the floor.

Oliver pulled the knife out of the fallen enemy. Two left.

The scuffle had not been without noise, nor had the creature died without cries. The cell door opened, and the other vampire peered out balefully.

Rapidly, Oliver brandished the cross. The vampire snarled, threw up a hand, retreated into the room. Oliver followed, crucifix held before.

The larger vampire opened its eyes wide to see the youth standing so in the doorway. Immediately, he felt the rays—and dodged away as far as he could.

Turner remained tied to the chair. Lord Billington slumped in a heap, oblivious to his surroundings.

Turner blanched, and emitted a whimper. His left side, and part of his back was to Oliver. "Quickly, lad. Cut me free. Then get rid of that cross, or it will hurt you as well!"

His parted shirt hung loose—and something was attached to his chest. What had they done to him? But there was no time for questions. Speedily, Oliver moved to Turner and sliced through his bonds. The vampires cringed against a silent terminal.

Once his hands were free, Turner immediately whisked them to his chest. There was a 'click'. He re-buttoned his shirt and turned to Oliver.

"What about the other ones?" he asked weakly.

"Dead."

"Penelope?"

"Waiting in the van."

"Okay. Now discard that cross. It may have done your hand damage already."

"You'll not escape," the leader said. "You'll—"

Flipping the cross-knife over, Oliver re-gripped it by the blade, and flung it. The blade sank to its hilt in the vampire's eye. Blood spouted in a crimson fountain. Sparks flared. The creature screamed.

They did not linger to observe its death throes, but ran from the room, up the steps, and through the hallway. The other vampire pursued, on their heels like a malevolent shadow.

They clattered through the drawing room, knocking over furniture. Oliver could hear the remaining vampire behind him, and urged Turner to increase his speed.

They flung the front doors open and hurtled through. The van waited for them, open. They leaped aboard and crashed the rear hatch closed, then Turner moved swiftly to the controls and started the engine. He eased the hand-brake off, engaged the gears.

They ripped through the night, spattering the last vampire with loose gravel flung up from the spinning wheels.

"You know, we *could* stop and finish that one off," Oliver suggested. His shirtfront was streaked with blood, as were the backs of his hands. His muscles ached. He realized that he was shaking uncontrollably. Grabbing the counter, he held onto it until the shudders stopped.

Penelope tumbled wearily onto the cot, which squeaked in protest. "Leave *me* out of it. I had one hell of a time getting those gates open. They're *heavy!*"

"No. We'd best not," Turner replied to Oliver while leaning toward the windshield and trying to discern the new twists and turns that the headlights were discovering in the road. "God knows what other *things* they've got lurking about that wretched castle." His voice was hoarse with exhaustion. "If you feel so peppy, lad, how about driving this thing a little distance more. By my reckoning the dawn's only an hour or two distant." He eyed the quivering needles of his meters. "Hmm. Batteries not as strong as they might be. We'll have to make a brief stopover in Exeterton to charge them."

"But that's north," Oliver said. "I thought we were headed west."

"That's what I thought too," Turner said, slowing to a halt so that the youth could take the controls. "Until Satan told me where the spaceship landed."

"He *knows!* And he *told* you?"

"Thought he had me, didn't he? Thought I was to

be brain-wiped by that machine in the dungeon, sucked
dry of myself as those vampires suck blood from men.
So he couldn't help boasting. I don't think he's managed to figure how the ship can be opened, but he's
found it."

"Penelope!" cried Oliver. "Did you hear that? We
found it!"

But the woman was silent, still prone on the cot,
wearing a thoughtful expression.

"Penelope?"

"Oh," she said, finally, blasé. "Where did you say
it was? And how are you *sure* he's not found a way in?
The whole trip might be a waste."

"It's not two hundred miles distant, in the Valley
of Starlight, which is situated in the Mountains of
Jewels. Only three days travel, including stopovers, I'd
say. As for getting into the thing . . . well, although
Satan's technology is the most advanced on this world,
I can tell you it won't be a drop in the bucket com-
pared to the technology of a civilization able to travel
through space. He won't be able to pierce any defenses
—not even a cracked hull."

"You know an awful lot, Mr. Turner," Penelope
said, shifting position on the cot to regard him. Her
voice carried a trace of coy admiration.

"I have an extensive collection of books available
to me back at HOPE headquarters," Turner said, settling his ample rump in a chair. "But perhaps we can
discuss such subjects—including your background, my
dear, once we've a little rest inside us."

Penelope agreed readily enough, a shrug in her voice.

As dawn fingered the sky, exhaustion finally over-
came Oliver. He pulled the van to the side of the road
and slept. Among his dreams was a replay of Turner's
rescue. And again, he wondered what Turner had done
to his chest. What were the vampires about to do to
him?

Abruptly, Oliver awoke.

A hand was on his shoulder, shaking him.

His eyes opened to see Penelope, beautiful Penelope,

stooping over him, forefinger to lips. "Shh," she whispered. "Quiet. I want to show you something, Oliver. Something I've suspected ever since I met your Geoffrey Turner."

"What?"

She shushed him again. He squinted at the bright windshield. Only midmorning. She pulled him up insistently, and led him to the rear of the van, where Turner lay curled in a deep sleep.

"I don't see anything unusual," Oliver complained in a sleepy whisper. "Can't this wait?"

She shook her head, knelt slowly at Turner's side, unblocking the sunlight which slanted from the windshield onto his massive form. Carefully, with both hands, she parted the ripped front of his white, ruffled shirt. On the hairy chest was etched the outline of an eight-inch square. The chalky skin at one corner was—bent back—but bloodlessly so. Bent back just far enough to reveal a softly blinking light and a short stretch of microminiaturized electronic components.

Once again, failure.

Success had been so close this time, so frustratingly close!

He had recorded it all to savor the long-sought victory so bizarrely denied him all these centuries.

And now that victory had been wrenched from his grasp.

He replayed the tapes in disbelief . . .

. . . and once again that fat, dark, bushy-haired face swam into view before him: Geoffrey Turner.

His servants had secured him by the machine. It was well that Turner's internal mechanisms did not lend him any kind of superhuman strength. The mandroid's superior innards were merely to give him longevity. And that had certainly succeeded.

"I've waited a long time for this," Satan heard his own electronic voice say.

"Five centuries, give or take a few decades," Turner replied.

"And at the most opportune *time. We have located the starship you seek, and are presently working on its destruction—there are no signs of life within. And you'll be interested to know, you were headed in the wrong direction. It lies to the north two hundred miles, in the Starlight Valley among the Mountains of Jewels. Much good that will do you now."*

"You always were a gloating bastard, Nicholas."

Nicholas! That accursed name again!

"You will not *call me that. My name is Satan!"*

"You really believe *that, don't you, old chap. They never straightened you out, really, on Bedlam. If only I'd not been outside the Computer when that message arrived. It* was *a message, wasn't it, Nicholas? From the Empire. Something had happened. Rebels, I dare say. And successful at that, or we'd have visitors by now."*

"You mouth absurdities, servant of God. You wish to confuse Me. But your God has deserted you—and you are within My power now. You have fought well, Turner, all these years. I've seen you only second hand many times, but only when you have destroyed My minions. Now it is My turn."

"Oh really, Nicholas. This is a bit melodramatic, don't you think? And you needn't call me Turner anymore. You know my real *name. And, down deep, you can't conceal the* truth *from yourself, can you? You're not Satan. You're just a particularly* mad *human being who, I must say, has outlived his time by several centuries."*

"Silence! I will bear this no longer."

"Very well. But what do you mean to do with me?"

Satan delivered orders to the leader of the vampires, the creatures he'd summoned to his personal chamber less than a week before. The somber fiend stepped forward and ripped open the front of Turner's shirt.

"As a servant of My Enemy, you have a peculiar spiritual body," Satan said.

"Spiritual? No. Absurd!" Turner cried. "It's flesh and electronic mechanisms, just like your three vam-

pires here. A little more flesh, perhaps. Not as strong. But the science that bore me is the same that bore your Computer. Can't you realize that, man!"

"I am not a man!"

A vampire advanced, scalpel in hand, and pried open Turner's chest.

"This is what We seek, Geoffrey Turner, as well as your life," Satan continued. "We mean to analyze the spiritual essence that so well augments your flesh, and has maintained your cumbersome body all these years. The mechanism before you is to thoroughly analyze your body in its present, living form. Then, Geoffrey Turner, you will be brought down to Hell where the body will be examined in detail. Only it will be a dead body, sucked dry of certain spiritual energies, which will be absorbed into me."

"I am not afraid of death," the fat man said. "My life has been well-spent, serving the ideals of my Queen, and my Empire."

"Such ridiculous claptrap. Farewell, Geoffrey Turner. Your soul's energy shall augment My life force. It shall burn in Hell forever with Me!"

Satan had ended the transmission there. He had planned to watch the proceedings through the screen, but simply could not. He did not even tune in through the vampires' faculties. It was too much to bear.

His mind boiled with confusion.

" . . . not my name . . . Turner . . . Geoffrey Turner . . . not my real name . . ." The phrase churned around and around in his mind.

Turner. Geoffrey Turner. Yes—of course that was the creature's name. What else could it be? He simply would not accept the idea that this could be . . . could be . . .

Absently, his thoughts keyed a sequence in the computer's memory banks.

Somewhere in the heart of the mammoth machine, a search was instigated, data located. In a long-forgotten maintenance station a hard-copy terminal coughed briefly and expectorated a paper rectangle. It read:

0110101000—MANDROID, HISTORICAL 010-
101111—TURNER, GEOFFREY 0110101000:
PRODUCTION OF HISTORICAL MAN-
DROIDS, SIMULACRUMS—ANDROIDS. PRO-
DUCTION BEGUN: 2105. FIRST PRODUCT:
PRINCE ALBERT, CONSORT TO HER MAJ-
ESTY, QUEEN VICTORIA. ANDROIDAL/
MECHANICAL CONSTRUCTS PROGRAMED
TO DUPLICATE ILLUSTRIOUS INDIVID-
UALS OF FIRST VICTORIAN EMPIRE. PUR-
POSE: HISTORICAL CONTINUITY BE-
TWEEN REIGNS AND ACROSS GALACTIC
EMPIRE. FURTHER INFORMATION: 0110-
101001—MANDROID, HISTORICAL: DIA-
CHRONIC HISTORY.

010101111—TURNER, GEOFFREY: PRES-
ENT PSEUDONYM OF HISTORICAL MAN-
DROID PRODUCED 2266 AD. LAST IMPE-
RIAL DUTY: SUPERVISION OF WORLD-
SCAPING OF PLANET STYX OF STAR
SYSTEM AZ108063. PREVIOUS NOTORIETY:
NOVELIST FAMED FOR WORKS OF SCI-
ENCE FICTION—'THE TIME MACHINE'
(1895); 'WAR OF THE WORLDS' (1898);
'FIRST MEN ON THE MOON' (1901)
FURTHER INFORMATION: 010101110 —
WELLS, H. (HERBERT) G. (GEORGE).

TEN

━━━━━━━━━━━━━━━━━━━━━━━━━━━━━

IT stabbed through him like a knife: hot, sharp fear.
Not simple fear for life, or fear of the unknown. No,
it was a more subtle fear, a paranoia. In the world that
was being revealed to him, who could he trust?

"My God! They must have switched a false Geoffrey
Turner for the real one!" was his first reaction. "But
how—and why?"

"No, Oliver. This is the same Geoffrey Turner who
doctored me just yesterday," Penelope said, shifting
her tousled hair from her eyes, which held a look of
smug satisfaction. "I thought there was something . . .
unusual about him. He's not human as you or I are,
Oliver. Not . . ."

Turner's heavy-lidded eyes flickered open, brown
pupils large. They focused on the pair hovering over
him, noticed the shocked expression on Oliver's face,
then darted to his open shirt. "Ah—should have fixed
that." He glanced up, chubby face wearing an expression more appropriate to a little boy caught with his
hand in the cookie jar. "Well. You know then." He

shrugged lightly, his rumpled clothes rustling. "I suppose it doesn't make a whole lot of difference. We're all in this together, aren't we?" He grinned at Penelope. "Even you, my dear." He reached up and touched Oliver's hand. "You're not . . ."

Oliver flinched, jerked the hand away, and moved back a step. "What—what *are* you?"

"Oh, dear boy, I do assure you I'm not a *what*. I'm quite as much a *who* as either of you, perhaps more so."

"But . . . you're what you call the nightcreatures . . . an android!"

"Mandroid, actually, Oliver. An historical mandroid, if you will. A simulacrum modeled after another man dead for centuries . . . and not much resembling him mentally or physically after all this time."

Oliver shook his head. "This . . . This is too much for me. I don't understand at all."

"I suppose I've some explaining to do if I want to keep you aboard."

"I should think so," Penelope said.

"No matter. I probably would have told you, Oliver, eventually. I don't know about her, though."

"I'm as much in this as you all are now," she said, airily, saucily placing her left hand on a well-rounded hip.

"You like adventure, eh?"

She smiled, a mysterious twinkle in her eye.

"But if you're an android—or mandroid, whatever . . ." Oliver blurted. "You must have been created by Satan. You must be . . ."

"Oh, stuff and nonsense, lad. Do you think if I served Satan I'd be on this mission? Of course Satan didn't create me. And do you think if I had an alliance with him I'd be traveling about, ridding this world of his minions these *centuries!*"

"Centuries!" Oliver's eyes widened.

"Yes—if I'm to tell you part of the truth, I might as well tell you all of it. Lord help me, I need a drink. This is all a bit sudden." He rolled over, ponderously pushed himself up, and raided his already diminished liquor cabinet.

After a quick gulp of whiskey, he gazed back at them. "Yes. I suppose I should give you the entire story. But whatever I say will not change this journey one jot. I can tell you as we travel. We'd best get started if we want to make Exeterton by sundown. I've a feeling that old Satan is going to throw a good many of his forces our way, and I don't want to confront them at night. Here, let me wash up, and I'll tell you my story as I drive. All right?"

Still stunned, Oliver nodded. Penelope agreed eagerly. She seemed to be sucking all this in joyfully.

They attended to their separate toilets speedily, took a breakfast of fruit and cheese from the cabinet. They ate as they traveled.

After the last crunch of a bright red apple, Geoffrey Turner told them of the grand and glorious Second Victorian Empire.

By the year AD 2039 of Homeworld, Earth, that place of the origin of mankind—now scattered among the stars—had developed a cohesive world-wide civilization. Somehow, the wars had stopped long enough to homogenize the race of Man into a semblance of unity with a world government of sorts and a network of all of the large computers that ran the world.

The sun never set on that vast, worldwide computer.

And one day it became sentient. An intelligence was generated from among the countless neurodes that held all the information and knowledge of all the ages past.

A being was born, but a slightly incomplete being, one lacking identity. Built to serve Man, each of its segments was oriented humanistically. Now it reasoned, lived, infinitely superior to any single human, and yet not *really*, for it had no conception of itself . . .

And therefore grew a little mad.

Somehow, in a manner never fully understood, the intelligent computer modeled itself, its identity, its basic thought-patterns, its basic ideals and beliefs, after a figure of Earth's past.

Queen Victoria.

"And she took over the Earth subtly, very subtly," Turner explained as Oliver and Penelope listened, enrapt. "She was wise enough to realize that blatant use of the tremendous force at her command—the *subjugation* of mankind—would be foolish. So she initiated trends, artistic, philosophical, political, all of which led to a renaissance of Victorian thinking. The pendulum of history was on her side—she rode the swing toward stricter morals, away from the tremendous freedom individuals of society had then.

"Of course, her activities took decades. But she was in no hurry—she was effectively immortal. And when the revolution came, not a shot was fired, nor a person killed. There was no coup as such. Over the years and under the careful guiding hand of the computer Victoria, society began to emulate British Victorian society. English became the standard language of the world— British English. The sort we speak now.

"And while all this was happening, Victoria was doing much to improve the worldwide space program. Before long, a method to speed travel to the stars was developed and habitable planets were discovered. As Victoria asumed the rule of Earth, a new Victorian Empire was formed."

Turner told them of that Empire.

He told of myriad worlds colonized with the seed of Man, of the sense of purpose each colonist bore within his breast, of a rekindling of Victorian optimism . . . A new era was at hand, one promising peace and prosperity for all.

He mentioned other life forms, intelligent aliens— some friendly and docile, some fierce, belligerent. Wars were fought—some lost, some won.

And into all this, over the course of the day's ride, he embroidered detail of the glory that was the Victorian Space Empire.

"Victoria was, of course, Earthbound. She was Empress of hundreds of worlds eventually, yet she could visit but one.

"She formed a simulacrum of Prince Albert. Of flesh and steel and synthetics it was, just as Satan's night-creatures are, just as I am. She formed one of the original Victoria as well, linked it with her computerself.

"That was early on in her career. After concluding that Albert was a success, she created more walking, talking, *thinking* and *living* models of eminent figures of Victorian history. Historical mandroids, they were called. They were designed to live a thousand years or more, constructed of a balance of flesh and synthetics, metals and plastics that would begin to wear only after centuries.

"I am one of the later models. My real name is Herbert George Wells—or rather, that was the name of the man of Victorian times after whom I was fashioned. For a time, I had many of his characteristics—starting, of course, with his appearance and structure. Mandroids were fashioned merely from records, of course, so I was not an exact duplicate. Indeed, a little over half of the original Wells' life was lived beyond the death of the fleshly Queen Victoria. The period was completely ignored. I was the *Victorian* H. G. Wells, the celebrated journalist and author of early works of science fiction. A seer into a dark future. A prophet of the terrible rages of progress. And in this guise, I served in whatever capacities Victoria wished. Over the years, of course, I became my own person—changed—but always to the new Victorians I was the demigod from the First Empire, H. G. Wells. And I wrote *new* works of science fiction." He chuckled ruefully, and sighed. Then continued:

"Styx was one of the later worlds discovered. And a very special world it was. Victoria decided that it would be transformed into a small resort colony modeled after medieval England—hence the castles. But also she decided that many modern conveniences would be on hand, but inconspicuous. The natural beauty of the world was preserved, but beneath it were modern mechanisms. Hence the Computer that once ran things, and to a certain extent still does.

"To model this paradise of a world completely after the Britain of old, Victoria had a Colonel Hedley Nicholas, released from Bedlam, a world which was devoted solely to the treatment of the mentally ill. Colonel Nicholas had been for years an admired planetscaper, one of the true geniuses in the field, until a defective Direct Memory Access teaching device trapped him for three days and nights in a three-minute lecture on the medieval concept of evil—damned contraption etched the images and concepts ineradicably into his brain.

"For a while, Nicholas acted as though he was possessed of a medieval demon. But after rigorous deprogramming on Bedlam, it was thought he was cured.

"To aid his project, and to watch over him, I was sent to Styx some five hundred years ago. He was in charge, I was second in command.

"And then, somehow, the Empire collapsed. For five years we'd been building castles, overseeing the arrival of colonists, establishing a society. I was out at one of the communities when suddenly transmission was cut off from the Computer Mountain. When I went personally to look into the matter, I found the access doors were locked. I could not get in, nor could I raise Nicholas on the radio. The mountain was as silent as a tomb.

"The communities, over the next few years, began to grow, flourish—there was that problem with the dukes, of course, but that's a story for another time." Geoffrey seemed vaguely uncomfortable. "However, I worked to keep the memories of the Empire in the people's minds, but as they immersed themselves in their private lives, in the idyllic existence that was to be had on Styx, they thought less and less of the old society, taught their children naught of its grandeur and glory. For twenty years or so, Styx experienced a Golden Age. I do admit that I had given up hope of further communication from the Empire or from the Computer, which had been completed, but not yet interfaced to the portions of the communities it was meant to control. I assumed that just as something wrong must have happened to the Empire, so something must have happened at Computer Mountain. But, as there was no way in, I could not go to check. I concluded that Nicholas surely was dead . . .

"But twenty-five years from the beginning of the Great Silence, as it was called then, the Dark Ages began. Strange, horrendous creatures began to roam the world by night. Powerful, evil creatures intent on death and destruction—vampires, werewolves, all manner of demons—suddenly came to life. And soon, monsters of medieval and Greek myths began to travel the countryside after sundown.

"The communities walled themselves up. They looked for an explanation for this plague of monsters upon the land and they found it in their religion, Christianity. These were the legions of the Devil, seeking bodies and souls to devour. That was what people believed.

"And soon the world was populated not only with medieval castles and communities. It was populated with medieval minds.

"There were five hundred communities during the Golden Age. There are fewer now as some were rapidly overrun by the nightcreatures. And I grew to be the only one who knew the real reason for what was happening, the only one who remembered the origins of Styx. There was little I could do. Though initially I had my followers, technicians and the like, as the generations passed, time eroded memory of the Empire, clergymen used the Nightworld for their own ends. Eventually, people just would not believe me.

"It did not take me long to discover the true nature of the nightcreatures or to discover their author, and what had become of him. Somehow, Nicholas had suffered a relapse of his mental disease—he thought he was *Satan*.

"I waited the years I thought it would take for Hedley Nicholas to die . . . keeping myself low, for I was sure he was still aware of my existence, and would want me promptly destroyed. For when *he* died, surely the nightcreatures would cease wreaking havoc and terror across the countryside by night.

"But he did *not* die. And there could only be one reason—somehow, the man had developed a symbiosis with the Computer. That Computer kept him alive. There were biological functions built into it for agricultural and animal-husbandry research—that much I knew. And it became obvious that Nicholas was using them in alliance with the robot manufacturing centers, to create the monsters with which he was populating the planet.

"The man was a raving lunatic, thinking himself Satan, the fallen angel! But his madness was a curse over all the planet.

"I changed my name. I gained weight, and grew my beard long. I managed to gain a foothold in the minds of a very small community—and I started HOPE."

"Everything you told me was a lie—about your early life?"

"Of course, Oliver. My standard story, lad. And, had I shown you my innards, you'd have jumped right out the van and not stopped running until you'd reached home. And I need you.

"Anyway, starting HOPE took me years. I had to build weapons to deal with the creatures. I had to educate my workers. I had to move about the countryside, collecting books and followers. Most difficult, I had to change identities every twenty years or so, to prevent people from realizing I was not human in the same sense they were. They would have thought me a supernatural being as well—which I did not want at all . . .

"And so it has been, these past, weary five centuries. So weary that I have taken to drink. So weary that I thought I could not last much longer. But then, one night, I saw a shooting star. To the west. Only this meteor-streak did not fade. It remained strong and unvarying all the way to the ground. I'd seen such things before; it was a spaceship. There was yet a hope, and it rejuvenated me. That was a month ago. I set out in search of this spaceship . . . and now it is very close.

"It is the *one* hope I have to achieve what I have sought these many years. My one hope of ridding this world of Hedley Nicholas and his nightcreatures, of transforming Styx to what it was *meant* to be."

By the time Turner had finished his tale, the sun was near setting, and they were near Exeterton.

The van, dusty and bird-spattered, rattled over the rickety drawbridge spanning a fetid, algae-covered moat, then lumbered through thick, metal reinforced wooden gates after a brief and energetic exchange with a pair of bemused guards. However, once the armored sentinels had been assured that the carriage was not a Trojan horse from Satan, they were amiable enough, quickly reporting the strangers' arrival. The van was guided through a swarm of curious citizens to the mall at town's center, whereupon the representatives of community authority swept down with reserved welcoming hand-shakes and hospitality.

Might they weather the night here, and recharge their vehicle?

Of course! the town chiefs replied. You are our guests.

Upon learning that Oliver was the son of a Viscount they had heard of, special considerations were accorded the adventurers, including individual accommodations in the old castle's mossy keep.

Oliver no longer knew what to make of Turner. The revelations had almost been too much for his mind to encompass—it took what was left of the shreds of his former world-view, and blew them away; away across the empty spaces between the now cold, cold stars.

Walking back to his room from a refreshing evening bath during which he had reflected on Turner's tale, Oliver peeked into the man's narrow chambers.

Turner sprawled, big belly up, on the plump four-posted bed. A small candle flickered and dripped yellow wax by his side. An empty green bottle lay overturned on the carved hardwood side-table, a puddle of red wine below its gaping mouth. Geoffrey Turner slept, snoring sonorously.

Strange. This man was not all flesh and bone. He had lived over five hundred years. He knew things Oliver had never dreamed of, had traveled space, had seen much of his beloved Empire.

Turner was born of a machine. His insides were a mesh of flesh and mechanism. Yet he was as human as any man Oliver had ever met.

Perhaps more so. What was it like, living so many years apart from the civilization that created you? Oliver decided that Turner's mind must have been terribly intent on his goal to have survived, sane, all these years.

What sorts of doubt must quiver in Geoffrey Turner's mind? Oh, he usually sounded bluff and self-assured in his basic humanity, but every so often, Oliver realized, there had been hints of troubled thoughts, even of pain, in the man's brown eyes. And, also, there was the drinking . . .

Perhaps just as this Hedley Nicholas lived in a Hell, so did Geoffrey Turner.

Only Turner had not made *his* Hell.

Troublesome thoughts buzzing, Oliver slipped the door shut and tiptoed down the corridor, passing Penelope's quarters. A rectangle of dim light slid under her door. She was still awake.

He eased the brass-knobbed door open, glanced in. Penelope sat at a mahogany desk in the far corner of the gray plaster-welled room. She wore a soft, smooth, blue silk nightdress that the Viscountess of Exeter had provided. Quite intently, she bent over a piece of brown paper, scribbling and scratching with a thin pencil. Mouth creased into a serious frown, she wrote hastily, not noticing that Oliver watched her.

She had a fog-smeared window overlooking a mist-shrouded mews cracked open slightly. A motley assortment of thatched and slate roofs, lightning rods, crooked spires and odd-shaped chimney pots sprouted beyond the window like the landscape in a surreal cemetery.

A night breeze gently caressed the long, newly-washed golden splash of Penelope's hair where it kissed the delicate slope of her cream-colored shoulders. She was propped so that the sweeping gown pulled tight over her back, accentuating her graceful lines.

Something ached in Oliver as his eyes sucked in the sight of her. Never before had he met a woman like her, anywhere. She was as fresh, as vibrant as a spring day in Fernwold's Forest. And strong, mysterious . . .

Seeming to sense his lingering gaze, she turned, saw him. A smile curved her moist lips, a kindly gleam came to her eyes.

"I saw your light. I thought we might talk," Oliver said softly.

"Of course." Penelope gestured to a nearby chair, then to herself. "If you'll excuse the informal attire . . . although I suppose you've seen me in worse . . ."

"You said you'd realized that there was something unusual about Geoffrey when you first met him," he said, sitting down. "You seem to know quite a lot. Much more than I do, at any rate."

"From my travels, Oliver. I do travel a lot, and there are bits of truth here and there, in books, in people's minds and legends."

"Then you can confirm what he had to say today—his story?"

She shrugged. "Here and there. It *does* conform to what Lord Billington had to say . . . and Turner's reaction to that."

"Yes. Yes, come to think of it, it does." He looked away, thoughtfully, then turned back to regard her quizzically. "But how can you take it all so calmly?"

She smiled easily, leaned over, and patted his knee. "It's been hard for you, hasn't it—these past days."

"Yes," he acknowledged.

He looked deep in her liquid blue eyes, but saw nothing there save for his own doubled reflection.

"You're strong, Oliver," she said in a whispery voice. "I can see that quality in you, deep within. I *do* like you." She stretched out her graceful hand, took his, smiled again with an evocative twist of her lips. "I think now you'll wonder if unusual people you meet are entirely human, and not partially electronic like our Mr. Turner."

"You've not told me your plans, Penelope."

"Goodness. To travel along with you, of course, I'd very much like to see this spaceship."

"I'm not sure. . ."

"That Geoffrey Turner would care for that much? No. Perhaps not. But *you'll* let me, won't you?"

"Of course. As far as I'm concerned, you're quite valuable to us."

"Thank you." She stood, swept back her hair, pulled Oliver up. The scent of roses and violets clung about her. "Come here, Oliver," she said, guiding him over to the window, parting the ebony floor-length curtains more. "Tell me what you see in the sky."

The night was clear. Stars speckled the rich black, obscured only by an occasional wisp of cloud.

"Stars of course," he replied, not understanding.

She tossed back the silvery fall of her hair, slid her body against his. Her supple hands stroked his back. Her breasts were firm against his chest. Her hair brushed his face; it was full of her intoxicating fragrance. Nuzzling his ear with her perfect nose, Penelope breathed a whisper: "Think about those stars, Oliver."

And, as suddenly as she had embraced him, she backed away, eyes wide and alive. "And think of *me*, Oliver Dolan." Those eyes seemed to flash with an urgent azure fire that sped a tingle through him. She grasped him firmly by his arm, gently walked him to the door. "But, alas, I've some work to finish yet tonight, while it's fresh in my mind. And you need your rest." She smiled wickedly, then kissed his cheek quickly before closing the door. "There will be time enough, dear Oliver," her throaty voice came through the closing door. "There will be time."

He went to bed more baffled than ever, finding her command to think of her not difficult at all.

ELEVEN

CURIOUSLY, Oliver found it unnecessary to convince Turner that Penelope should accompany them. Indeed, the fellow seemed to expect that she would.

Rising early, the company ventured forth, with good wishes from their hosts, into a crisp, resplendent fall day and onto the north road. The recharged van fairly thrummed with power, and the wheels seemed to squeak with enthusiasm; the wooden veneer creaked in raucous counterpoint. An hour out they forded a shallow sparkling stream easily, and proceeded with good pace down a snaking highway bordered by wood and field.

Rested, Turner seemed quite at ease, and he rambled on about the Second Victorian Empire and his five centuries on Styx. The road north was unusually smooth; they were able to make good speed toward the rugged slopes of the Mountains of Jewels.

"These roads were built when Styx was planet-scaped?" Penelope asked.

"Yes. And maintained reasonably well over the years,

under the circumstances. Of course, the climate of Styx is mild worldwide, which helps."

"You've been all over this world, haven't you?" Penelope's questions were direct and specific, always. A very incisive mind, Oliver thought as he drove.

"Yes. All over. I've been to most communities."

Turner talked on, as Oliver pondered. He would have liked to consider Geoffrey Turner further, to puzzle out the enigma of—what had he called himself? An historical mandroid. But he found his mind—and when they were free of watching the road ahead, his eyes—wandering toward Penelope.

She grew more beautiful every time he looked at her. An incredible aura of mysterious promise garbed the woman. And when she met his gaze with smiling, knowing eyes, shivers danced down his spine.

Exciting shivers.

Still, entwining and intermingling with the reactions Penelope was causing, were questions about her which would not wear words, could not be formed into inquiring sentences.

He listened to Turner talk, as did Penelope, who sat attentively, taking it all in.

The travelers spent the night in Farleigh, a community in the foothills of the Jewels, even though some of its inhabitants were quite in an uproar over a van that moved without horses.

They spent a peaceful evening conversing with the Viscount and his counselors. Oliver wondered what these people would think if they knew they shared bread, wine, and talk with a man who had been created, rather than born. As he studied their faces, listened to their talk, he realized how truly backward they were in their thinking. Days before he had been the same way.

Strangely, he envied their ignorance.

Only one guest room was available, so they had to crowd into that together.

They retired early, Turner muttering worriedly about

an attempt on Satan's part to storm the community to
seize its guests.

"I've warned them to place extra guards," he said,
pulling the covers over himself. "I dare say Nicholas is
furious, and would very much like to have at me again.
I do hope he hasn't any more of those dragons."

"I shouldn't think so," Oliver commented. "The one
he sent to Fernwold was not even completed."

"Well, if there is an attack, I've informed the Viscount to just open the gates, and let us speed on our
way, taking the trouble with us. That is the safest alternative for us and them."

But there was no attack.

The rising sun found the community much as it had
been when it set the night before. The party breakfasted
quickly, disconnected the charging cable from the
mains, and, with a hurried word of thanks to their
hosts, departed into the Mountains of Jewels.

The sun barely over the horizon, Oliver could see
why the mountains were associated with gems. Huge
globules of dew hung from the branches of trees, sparkling like rare stones in the sun.

"Viscount Hartford says the Valley of Starlight is
some twenty-five miles distant. Impossible to reach in
a day by horseback, but I think we ought to be there
by late afternoon."

"You mean, there's a road through here?" Oliver
asked, wondering.

"Yes. In bad repair, but it *is* a road. It leads to
Royceford, 'on the opposite side of the mountains."

The sun rose higher in the sky, and burned the fat
dew drops away. Progress through the Jewels was not
as good as it had been on the old road; pot holes
abounded, crevices yawned. But, moving carefully, they
navigated it and eventually drew up beside the mountain which bordered the Starlight Valley.

"Right," Turner announced. "We'll have to park the
van here, and walk the rest of the way. Penelope, I

want you to carry this sack here, all right? We'll get some work out of you yet."

"And if we *can't* figure a way in . . ." Oliver said, trailing away from the obvious finish of the sentence.

Turner smiled confidently. "Oh, we'll get in."

The Styxian sun hung westering on the horizon, bracketed by two blunt-peaked mountains, when Geoffrey Turner, Penelope Reynolds, and Oliver Dolan crested the rise. The sunlight, filtered through more atmosphere and the wispy strands of clouds lacing the sky, had cooled, turned a reddish hue which gave the landscape an aura of a burnished gold. A faint breeze wafted the earthy odors of all into Oliver's nostrils— the musty smell of humus and dead leaves, the brisk scent of the pine trees which grew in abundance in the valleys and on the mountainsides. Birds chirped everywhere save when the party passed. Occasionally, a tame mountain wind, full of the clean mountain tastes, would gather dead leaves up into sprightly whirlpool dances.

Geoffrey Turner, abundantly and annoyingly optimistic, scanned the landscape, hand on portly hip, occasionally tiptoeing to a higher vantage point. Oliver kept abreast of him, nervously watching as the sun slid lower. They would not even have time to make it back to the van, he thought. But Turner *was* correct about most things, and evidently knew what he was doing. Hastily striding through the pathless forest, Oliver clutched his weapons defensively. He would be ready for anything. Behind them lagged Penelope, who had stoutly refused weapons. But whenever Oliver turned to reassure himself that she had not been lost, he caught her wearing an enigmatic smile. The woman seemed to be enjoying herself. Her spritely eyes radiated mirth, as though she was laughing at a silent joke she hated to share with her companions. Lithe arms folded over abdomen, accentuating her bust-line, she strode along confidently.

At the peak of a rise, Turner jogged forward hurriedly, halted, surveyed. Joining him, Oliver could see that they'd chanced upon a break in the foliage which permitted a full view of a bowl-bottomed valley, filled not with trees, but with a small grassy plain.

A plump arm streaked out, pointing. "Look!" Turner said excitedly. "My word, I can see it from here!"

Oliver craned his neck high to obtain Turner's point of view.

And there it was indeed, nestled on the near side of the plain like a bright silver egg. A huge *metal* egg, roughly twice as long as it was high, resting on its side. Oliver found himself a bit breathless to get a closer look at it, and lost his fear of descending into the valley as the sun left it. He was caught up in the thing's silver sparkle.

Geoffrey Turner was from another world, but somehow *he* did not align properly with Oliver's sense of otherworldliness. Turner was, after all, Turner. Perhaps more than a man, perhaps not. But his home was obviously Styx—he looked it. But the spaceship—*that* caused his skin to goose-pimple. "Penelope. He's right. The spaceship! Have a look!"

"Oh yes," said the woman, coolly. "So *there* it is."

They began the descent toward it with renewed speed.

As they puffed up beside the craft at little less than a run, the sun was little more than a golden sliver on the horizon. Oliver had bounded past the others and was running toward the nearer end of the ovoid. The lad was within yards of its mirror-smooth surface when Turner cried out "I think . . ."

Slowing immediately to a fast walk, Oliver looked back . . . and struck something.

Early stars seemed to slash the sky. Oliver realized his eyes were closed. He opened them, and found himself lying prone in the high grass.

"Ah, I *thought* as much," Turner clucked, drawing up to Oliver's side and helping him to his feet. "A force-field. Good protection, that. I doubt if Satan's got anything to pierce it. You okay, Oliver?"

"Yes, but what? . . ." Weaving, Oliver righted himself and regained his balance.

"A shield of protective energy radiating about the hull of the ship to prevent access. A defensive measure, used in space as well, I might add, though probably with a denser shield. Yes, if you look at it right, you can see the glimmerings of energy."

Yes, there *were* fuzzy shimmers when the otherwise invisible field was looked at sidewise against the setting sun.

"Ah, yes," Turner said, pointing toward the opposite end of the spacecraft, about fifty yards away. "Over there—that ditch." A large hole was dug just outside the perimeter of the forcefield. "They've tried to dig a hole *under* the field. Little good that will do them. Even if they *should* somehow pierce the screen, Lord knows the hull is probably composed of an alloy they can't hope to break through. No, I'd say that this ship is fairly impervious to intruders."

"But *someone* must have landed it here. Where *are* they?" demanded Oliver.

Penelope drew up with them. "All right, Herbert Wells or Geoffrey Turner or whoever you are. How do you propose to get us through this forcefield, as you call it, and through the incredibly strong alloy of this ship's hull?"

"I haven't the faintest idea," the fat man said brightly.

"My God!" Oliver cried. "Nightworld is just about on top of us, a whole *slew* of nightcreatures is going to be here in a few minutes, and you haven't the faintest idea of how we're going to get safely *inside* this vessel?" Had the fellow lost his wits? Oliver looked toward Penelope for support, but the woman seemed totally unfazed.

"Dear boy, I didn't say that we wouldn't get in. I merely noted that I've no power to get us through either the forcefield or into the starship."

"But surely you're familiar with the things—you've ridden in them," said Oliver, desperately.

"Of course. But this is quite a different model and type of spaceship from those I was accustomed to."

"Then do you propose that we just stand here, and let Satan's beasts have us?"

Turner shrugged. "That's up to Penelope here, isn't it, dear girl?" His head shifted to her inquiringly.

Penelope's quiet smile turned into a loud grin. "How did you know, you ancient fox?"

"Perhaps it would be best if I let you in on that, when we're in the ship. Oliver's right. The sun *is* about down, and I've no doubt Satan has a crew of his minions hard at work here from dusk to dawn. I'll leave it to your imagination what will happen if they find us here so pitifully outnumbered."

With a curt nod, Penelope strode to the forcefield. Pulling back her sleeve, she revealed a slim, shiny black bracelet, waved it in the air, then held it steady. "All right," she announced. "Quickly walk after me. I've pulsed a twenty second aperture." She walked across the stretch of grass without encountering the invisible wall. Turner hastily scampered behind her, Oliver following, astonished.

"Did you have company on your trip?" Turner inquired as they walked behind Penelope, who was striding around to the other side of the vessel.

"No. Just me," she answered without turning around.

"Penelope!" Oliver said. *"You're* the owner of this spaceship. *You* came here from the Empire."

"You catch on fast, Oliver," she responded as she stopped before a seemingly unbroken stretch of smooth, silvery metal. "Only it's not an Empire. That idiocy was dissolved centuries ago. It's a confederation of planets now. I don't represent that confederation."

Again she raised the black bracelet, waved it. A seam cracked the slick metal. The split widened, slid back to reveal a corridor. A ramp tongued forward and settled to the grassy surface of the plain. Bright light spilled from the interior onto the twilit field. "Welcome to the *Orion,* my friends. Do hop aboard, and make yourselves at home."

TWELVE

THE experience was like entering another world.

A world of streamlined coolness, of symmetry, of geometrical perfection.

Oliver, used to the shabby comforts of Styx' Victorian architecture, accustomed to the irregularities of nature's forms, was shocked by the sleekness of it all, the sterile faultlessness.

Through a startlingly straight corridor they moved, silently. Up a short distance in a tightly curling stairway, they followed Penelope, whose movements were confident, accustomed as she was to the surroundings.

She stopped in a hemispherical room which bubbled out into other compartments. Here, she motioned them to be seated in any of a number of soft, smooth-covered chairs.

"Please. Make yourself comfortable." She made an encompassing gesture. "My lounge. How do you like it?"

"Fine," Turner said, plopping onto a length of cushion without hesitation. He unslung his weapons, placing them on the dull metal grid-work floor. "I must admit,

162

that little trek was a bit tiring for these old bones, muscles and mechanisms."

Mouth ajar, Oliver stared about the room. Bizarrely shaped green plants fringed walls hung with paintings that appeared three-dimensional. One portrayed an obviously alien landscape with jungle-type flora in the background, and a monstrous being with four eyes and snaking tentacles in the foreground. Penelope followed his gaze. "A grizoway, Oliver. From Tempest, a planet of the Rigel system. Do have a seat. You make me feel uncomfortable, standing."

Absently, Oliver sat down on a beige chair opposite Turner, still staring about. Immediately, he felt as if he had sat on something, a pet perhaps; then he realized the chair was responding to his body, reforming itself to his contours. Marvelously comfortable, if at first unsettling.

"Drinks?"

Turner requested something alcoholic.

Oliver did not know what to ask for. Penelope realized his discomfort. "No worry. I have something that I'm sure you'll enjoy."

Penelope strode blithely to a blue panel in a pink wall, did a spritely finger-dance over a series of buttons. After only a moment, a door slid open. She extracted a small tray upon which sat three bulbous containers. After distributing these, she settled onto a cushion, folding sleek legs together, and punched a set of controls on a small oval table. Soft, soothing music flowed from the walls, enveloping them in aural comfort. Oliver had never heard such sounds before, but thought they were quite nice.

And so was his drink. The liquid had the sweetness of peach-blossom scents, underlaid with a stimulating tartness. His tense muscles began to unwind as he felt himself relax. It was as if he had just consumed a decanter of wine.

"Now then, my friends," Penelope said after sipping a quantity of her own beverage and sighing languidly.

"And I do hope you'll consider me your friend. I feel I owe you an explanation. You've been quite liberal with explanations of yourselves . . ." she eyed Turner amusedly, ". . . in the long run, and I have dissembled abominably, loading your ears with vague fictions. But I wasn't sure that I could truly trust you. I lost my weapons when I lost my horse. At that point, all I wanted was to return safely here."

Turner lifted a hand. "Hold it. Let's start at the beginning. *Why* did you come here?"

"Very well. But first you promised to let me know how you saw through my guise. I thought I did rather well."

"Oh, you certainly *did*. Oliver didn't see through you, did you lad?"

"How *could* I?"

"Quite." Turner held out his hands expansively. "But I, on the other hand, have considerably more experience. I am well acquainted with all the peoples of Styx, with their manners, their customs, their modes of speech and accent. Yours, of course, conformed to none of these. Also, your acting was not *entirely* up to snuff. You tried to play the average Styxian young lady, clever, but vulnerable and innocent. However, a young woman of your obvious competence and experience cannot hide it. The way you handled yourself with that vampire—Oliver told me about it. Your fighting methods are not among those practiced on Styx. The very fact that you wished to accompany us told me something."

"Yes. Of course," she said with a wry smile. "I was so busy trying to determine who *you* were, really, that I failed to realize I was revealing myself to you.

"By the way, Penelope Reynolds is just a name I assumed for purposes of traveling about on your planet. My real name is Anziel Dubrelicy." She gazed at Oliver warmly. "You may call me Anzi."

"And you've come to contact the peoples of Styx?" whispered Oliver hopefully. "And you mean to help them against our Enemy?"

"I come to do nothing of the sort, Oliver," she said softly but firmly. "I came merely for a lark. A bit of adventure, if you will."

Turner's brow beetled. "I don't understand."

Anziel laughed musically, sweeping back her lustrous hair with merriment. "The great Geoffrey Turner for once dumbfounded?"

"I do admit, I thought you might be a representative of the current Galactic government, come to reopen contact with this rather remote world. I'd hoped that you were of a revived Empire, but I can see now that I hoped for far too much. A lark, you say. Adventure. You're an explorer?"

"No, not exactly. This ship is a pleasure craft owned by my father, an extremely wealthy machazoid trader. Dear daddy has a lot of power. I'm his spoiled-brat offspring, and he lets me have pretty much what I wish. On and off, I work for a star-media channel. I do offbeat stories for them. I came here to this world for such a story." Her eyes flashed enthusiastically. "And goodness, do I have one! A living relic of the stodgy Old Empire battling the Forces of Evil, his brave young assistant by his side. And what an Evil! Satan incarnate, with troops of blood-curdling monsters! Such forceful, primitive melodrama! Such a juicy story! How fortunate I was to run across the dusty records of this world in my researches. The Confederation hasn't bothered to stick its nose into this sector. Too busy developing on our own. But once I unleash my story, this place will be the most talked-about planet in the universe! Goodness, we'll all be stars, supercelebs! You, Turner—or Wells, rather—can sell your life's story to the feelies! Oh what grand cinema that will make. And you, Oliver—such an innocent! Your darling face will be in the minds of every teebop in the human universe. And your naivete—why the people of the Confederation will *love* you, dear boy! We'll all be rich!"

Oliver was stunned. Forgotten, his drink sat beside him. His mind reeled, unable to understand what exactly this woman was saying and not really wanting to.

Turner frowned deeply. "Just a moment, Anziel. You're running ahead of yourself."

"Am I? I suppose I am, aren't I? I do babble on sometimes, but can't you see I'm *excited?* Thrilled at the possibilities present by Styx, for *all* of us! Can you glimpse it, Geoffrey Turner? You'll be *free* of this little planet from now on! You'll be famous, a genuine curiosity. All the historical mandroids were destroyed by the rebels. You're the *only one left!* And Styx! Why, it's a living museum, not merely of the Empire Victoria created, but of the medieval world! And with a *real* force of darkness, keeping alive an antiquated form of Christianity! Absolutely *precious!* The Styxian sky will be full of peepies following the action and exploring all the really bizarre and wonderful nuances of life here. Styx will be the *rage!*"

"Just a moment. Let's go over this again," Turner said, sitting up rigidly, brown hair jostling. "You mean to tell me that you're here entirely on your own?"

"Well, I mentioned where I was going to my father. If I don't show up back home soon, they'll certainly send other starships."

"Why did you bother to endanger yourself by personally exploring the land?" the fat man asked softly.

"Oh, it really wasn't a danger, until my horse threw me, and sped away with the protection stored in my bags. I had a miniforcefield, laser guns, a few other weapons you wouldn't be familiar with, I'm afraid. I was safe. I just wanted to explore the countryside for myself. It was awfully exciting."

"And you want Oliver and me to go back to the Confederation with you?"

"Why yes, of course."

"What about Satan?"

"Excuse me?"

"I said, what about Satan? Don't you intend to aid us in destroying him, and ridding this world of the menaces that have stalked it for centuries?" Turner's face was red, flustered.

"My goodness, no. Of course not. Why, that would

ruin *every*thing. Why, no one would believe my story. And we'd lose the chance of televising this whole crazy business down here. And the pleasure of actually seeing the way life is *lived* here. You know, I was just thinking. We could set up a tourist board for this planet. Visitors can travel about just as I did, without letting on who they are, or where they're from, to the inhabitants. Such excitement! We can charge a *fortune* to the jaded citizens of the Confederation!" She hugged herself with exhilaration. During the course of her speech, her previous accent had entirely vanished into a more blunt, less pleasant tone.

The final rug had been pulled from under Oliver, and all below him now was empty space.

His mind drifted without borders, without direction. All seemed senseless. Purposeless. Against the greater backdrop of her civilization, Styx seemed ludicrous.

"But Penelope . . ." he began weakly, trying to return his mind to some sort of straight track.

"Anzi, Oliver. *Do* call me Anzi from now on. I've come to loathe 'Penelope'. We forgot all those awful Empire names long ago."

"Anzi. Don't you see—we've *got* to destroy Satan!" He hoped to sound emphatic, but the words rolled off his tongue lifelessly.

"Why?" she demanded. "The poor bugger's been terrorizing this world for five hundred Styxian years now. Will a few more make any difference?"

"I think I've got something here that might change your mind," Turner announced, digging into his backpack.

"Oh really?" said Anziel Dubrelicy, leaning forward with interest. "By all means show it to me, but I don't think . . ."

Geoffrey Turner pulled out a pistol, aimed it directly between her eyes. "Yes," he said. "I think you will find this little item *most* persuasive."

"This is really *too* barbaric!" Anziel protested as Turner signaled her to open the control room door.

"You really wouldn't *use* that thing, would you? I mean, you don't know anything about running this craft."

"Dare you take that risk, Anziel? This ship is not *entirely* different from a Victorian starship. It might take a while, but I'd learn."

Feeling numb, Oliver followed them into the spacious bridge when the access door whisked open. He barely noticed the banks of controls, the star-maps that hung in the room's center, the wonder of the room itself. He was just too stunned to take it all in.

Turner busily instructed Anziel, emphasizing the orders with waves of his weapon.

"Yes. This ship is quite capable of taking off and landing where you request. But why?" Anziel asked, pouting now.

"The mountain we'll land beside is the location of the world-computer, which is where Satan happens to be located."

"You're just as mad as he is, Turner." She stabbed buttons, adjusted levers furiously. A touch to a dial brightened the formerly dark surveillance screens. The pictures focused. One revealed a large party of night-creatures digging deeper below the ground surface beside the forcefield. The sky was clear, the stars glittery. The two moons shone bright.

"Mad? No, not mad, though Heaven knows I've every right to be. Five hundred years, Anziel. Five hundred years I've lived on this planet, my sole purpose for survival to *fight* those loathsome things you see trying to burrow their way in here. How old are you? No more than twenty-four, by my estimate. Have you an inkling of what it's *like* to live five centuries? To have this ponderous body belly through day after day of its attenuated existence, tolerate this petty pace of time? Would that I only had a normal span of life, and knew that that life was well-spent, opposing the forces which mar this world from the perfection idealized by she that created me. But no. A baker's dozen lifetimes I've fought my way through, keeping the ideals of the Empire alive, serving it even though I had strong suspicions it had dissolved in the ever-consuming vats of entropy which erode all that is good and right and grand in this Universe."

His voice choked with emotion.

"I can tell by the way you look at me you think me subhuman. A machine with a few shreds of flesh attached. Would that I were. Would that my thoughts did not own a being to think them. I've suffered more than any man has ever suffered, for I've suffered *longer*. I've gone through times of doubt and despair to which I'd not subject the worst criminal in the universe. Satan may live in his Hell, but my Hell lives in me.

"All that has kept me going, kept me from destroying myself, has been the driving force inside me that was kindled by the Queen. A force that strives for order and justice and balance. This was once a perfect world, a paradise. A world without conflict or physical unhappiness. That changed many years ago, and I vowed to myself that I would change it back however long it took, whatever it cost.

"It was *my* responsibility to ensure that nothing went wrong with Styx. If anything went askew with Nicholas, I was to be there to stop him. I was *not* there. I was outside the Computer, dallying with a village woman."

He chuckled humorlessly. "Yes, that should prove I'm human enough. You see, if I let you do exactly what you want to do, all these years of strife and pain will have meant nothing. They are losing their meaning even now, as I consider the implications of the upsetting words you've uttered."

"But don't you see, Turner, you've got *years* left. Don't you understand that you're a bigger person than this small, peculiar planet needs? The *Universe* deserves a look at you."

"This damned Universe deserves *nothing!*"

"You can have *anything* if you play your cards right," she urged.

"All I want is a climax to these decades upon decades of struggle. An end that will finally lend my life some dignity, that will appease the tremendous guilt that weighs heavily upon me. I can't stop thinking about all those generations of Styxian people, who have lived in fear and ignorance because of what *I* failed to do.

"I mean to destroy Satan. And I now have the means. I don't intend to give that up for some empty, meaningless promise from an apparently empty, meaningless civilization."

Oliver listened, and his confusion lifted slightly. It was well that he had gone with this man, no matter what came of it, even though he had to ascend through several layers of illusion to the stark reality of existence, of Styx against the vastness of the universe. He looked at Turner, who was trembling with anger and resolve. Oliver decided that any doubts of Turner's humanity were unjustified. He felt a sharp pang which he recognized to be a sort of love for the man.

Anziel shrugged. "Well, there goes *zillions* of credits. I never should have let you aboard."

"You *did,* and now you see that I'm intent upon my goal, and willing to kill you to get to it. Not that I want to at all, but any false move, Anziel, and it will be *you* who pulls this trigger."

She sighed, and gave Oliver an entreating, meaningful glance. But he looked away.

"Okay, Turner," she said. "It's your game now, I suppose. The ship's computer has generated a detailed hologlobe . . ." She flicked a switch and the tank-like enclosure before them was suddenly occupied by a sphere featuring a roughly equatorial land mass that wound around it like a snake. "Complete with co-ordinate system." She hit another switch, twisted a knob. Intersecting lines swept the globe. "Just give me the approximate coordinates so I'll know which way we're headed, and I'll take you there. Under *strong* protest."

After studying the globe for a moment, he supplied her with the necessary number. This she keyed into the computer, along with a brief flight plan.

"Okay. We'll just lift up on the antigravs and drift along about a kilometer above the surface. It's not a terribly great distance. It'll take us . . ." Quickly, she pecked in figures, hit a key, and a number flashed on a screen. "About two and a half hours."

"Do you mean to attack by night, Geoffrey? Surely the daytime would be better . . ."

"Oh, indeed it would, lad. But we'd have to wait the night, and I wouldn't trust our host here while I slept. No, it really doesn't matter. I might remind you, Oliver, that while it's night here, it is day elsewhere on Styx. I'm sure that Satan's *defensive* forces will be just as strong by day as they are now."

Anziel motioned them toward chairs. "I'd advise you to strap yourselves in for the ride. It won't be entirely smooth."

"Just remember what's pointed at your head all the while," Turner reminded her.

"How can I forget?" She settled down in the pilot's chair, tapped the necessary message into the ship's computer, and soon the craft rose, mightily confusing the nightcreatures below.

After they had reached the proper altitude, Oliver stared in wonder at the moonlit landscape far below. But another screen showed the stars and the moons to be no closer than they had ever been.

Followed by a dull booming sound, the spaceship streaked toward Computer Mountain and Satan's Hell.

THIRTEEN

THE ship's bridge held the quiet of a tomb through most of the journey. A charged quiet, pregnant with unvoiced emotion. Anziel, her angry eyes fixed on the myriad controls, stewed in frustrated fury. Geoffrey Turner, attention and pistol unwavering from Anziel, radiated an intensity of purpose. Oliver Dolan slouched limply, harnessed into a spare command module, the silence of vague despair about him, the silence of an inner struggle.

The recent past had slashed at him with unsettling speed. As he gazed at the stars, he knew the *pain* of the possibility that there was no God beyond them. The agony of the possibility that the Universe was a random collection of events. This had occurred to him earlier in the course of the revelations about the true nature of Styx's reality, but now that he knew the truth in its fullness, it was difficult to perceive a guiding, Godly hand behind it—only the erratic movements of chaos.

It dawned on him then—throwing a totally rational light upon the subject—that whatever meaning there was to life, *he* would have to find it, he alone. He had clung stubbornly to the womb of his religion, a belief that he had not chosen to be brought up in. And now he had been rudely ejected from that safe, warm place into a terribly cold and lonely exile of the spirit.

He was totally alone in himself. He felt that now, knew that. He alone was the author of his actions and decisions. He alone was the bearer of responsibility for those actions and decisions.

He had never before felt so alive.

But this new consciousness was the most frightening experience he had ever endured.

The screens showed mountains below, tall and ghostly in the moonlight.

Turner pointed. "That one," he said in a hoarse whisper.

Silently, Anziel nodded, keyed instructions. The craft descended, landed with a faint thump at exactly the site Turner had indicated.

Before them arched gates that glowed like silvery starlight.

"All right, Anziel. Very good," Turner said as he unfastened his metal-studded belts, keeping his gun trained on the woman. "Now, there are a few more things that I'll require of you."

She turned a fiery gaze upon him, spoke in a barely contained voice: "And what may they be?"

"You have personal weapons aboard, do you not? You mentioned laser guns, individual forcefields. Those would do quite nicely, I think."

She nodded. "I have a few weapons remaining, but I've no personal forcefields left."

"And I know this ship has defense mechanisms— the forcefield, for example. How about offensive weapons?"

"Of course not . . ." she started to say, but Turner interrupted her.

"Think carefully before you lie, dear Anziel. As I say, I can finish it myself—after I shoot you."

"A couple of lasers in the port bow, nothing heavy, though," she said.

"That will do. The computer's gates were not built to withstand any sort of modern assault."

"But what about defensive lasers?"

A smile played briefly over Turner's features. "My dear, if Satan had had laser power, most of this world would be a cinder. No, the World Computer of Styx was not programmed with either defensive or offensive mechanisms. Satan was limited to his own knowledge and that held by the Computer, which was quite slight in weaponry. Styx was to be a world of peace, not of war."

"I needn't ask what I'm to do with my laser, I suppose." She glanced at the screen which held a close-up view of the gates.

"No. I'll tell you. I want you to blast through them. They've stood between me and Nicholas for five hundred years. I want to see them melt to slag." His eyes smoldered as he glanced at the gates, as though his gaze alone would melt them. "But first, we need better personal arms." He turned to face Oliver. "Oliver. Since I've met you, I've not always been totally truthful with you. I realize that you've suffered quite a bit with what you've learned—I've not been insensitive to that. You've aided me immeasurably. If not for you, I'd certainly not have reached this far." He shifted his girth from foot to foot as he talked. "I've no doubt that I can use your help again in finally destroying Satan. But you've done enough. If you should decide *not* to come with me, I'll understand."

"You mean you won't force him at gunpoint?"

"He's never had to," Oliver said. His unfastened seat belt clunked on the deck. Rising, he faced Turner. "I've committed myself to going all the way with you, Geoffrey. I must take the responsibility of that decision."

"You don't understand, lad. I'm releasing you from that commitment. You're free. You have to decide again. Anziel's information places an entirely new light upon the situation. Our way of life upon Styx is doomed whether or not we destroy Satan."

"No, Geoffrey. My goal and purpose, though they've shifted, have not changed. If I do not go with you, I'll never forgive myself. I'm coming."

Turner's eyes gleamed moistly. "Good man."

He swirled back to Anziel. "All right. You'll give us both weapons. And then I'll tell you exactly the way I want it to be."

Twin beams crackled out into the darkness, slashing into the granite-framed gates. The attack was the work of but a moment. The gates glowed a fierce red-orange against the black of night, then exploded.

"Right. Cut it," Turner commanded. Anziel lifted a finger from the button, engaged the safety lock to prevent an accidental discharge. The ruined doorway still glimmered molten red in the viewscreen, where it was bracketed by targeting guides. Tendrils of smoke curled like fleeing ghosts, translucent in the moonbeams.

"Now we wait?"

"Now we wait, my dear," Turner confirmed. His pistol lowered. Another weapon was holstered in the belt which hung over his left shoulder—a laser gun. A similar weapon rested against Oliver's right hip. The weapon was a streamlined affair with a firing stud rather than the trigger Oliver had seen on regular guns. He leaned forward in his seat, attempting to stare past the deep darkness of the newly-opened tunnel's maw.

"Are you sure they'll respond?" he asked.

Turner nodded slowly.

They waited quietly, tensely, while the glow dimmed.

"You've got the force screen on full?"

"Do you think I'm stupid, Turner? Of *course* I do!"

"Just checking," Turner apologized, his attention returning to the tunnel. His expression changed to one of excitement. "There! Do you see them? I thought Satan might have prepared a defense, just in case. For whatever good it will do!" His expression was full of anticipation.

Oliver squinted to make out what Turner had seen and finally noticed dim forms near the tunnel's mouth. The muzzle of some large gun pointed up.

"A cannon!" Turner cried with much amusement. "Let them shoot, Anziel. I want Satan to realize the uselessness of his defense."

Over the audio monitor came a terrific 'Boom!' The cannon muzzle belched fire—the explosive charge it propelled burst against the forcefield yards from the *Orion's* hull.

"Marvelous! Now, Anziel. Give them both barrels."

Two beams sizzled briefly, connecting with the cannon and the creatures controlling it. A momentary flash illuminated the tunnel far into the depths of the mountain, outlining the disintegrating forms of the cannon and the nightcreatures.

"Enough."

Anziel buttoned off the lasers once more. Smoke billowed from the aperture. Fires burned bright within. Died.

Abruptly, a whole stream of nightcreatures flowed from the tunnel.

Slavering werewolves stalked forward. Small, wingless dragons and monstrous striped snakes crawled and slithered. A whole menagerie of horrid beasts followed.

"Incredible!" Anziel muttered. "Surely Satan, or whatever his name really is, must know these things haven't a hope against us in the open!"

"You don't understand the man's psychology—or psychopathy, rather," Turner replied grimly. "He won't admit that anyone has might superior to his. His Satanic pride will not permit that. He *must* remain in character, to support his delusions. Just wait until all the beasts that are to emerge are properly placed."

The creatures continued to be spewed forth until Oliver estimated a hundred of the things had surrounded the ship. They were trying to claw and bash their way through the forcefield screen.

"I think all our guests are here, Anziel," said Turner. "You may begin the fireworks."

The woman murmured assent, adjusted the lasers, then depressed the button. Again, the beams stabbed, this time in a slow, sweeping pattern. They slashed and whipped at the creatures like scythes cutting wheat. Anziel had focused them to thin shafts of searingly bright light. It took but a few minutes. When Anziel finally doused the beams, not a single nightcreature remained whole. They lay about in smoking heaps, clawed arms here, severed legs there.

"I'd rip through the beasts a few more times. When we disembark, we don't want any nightcreatures meeting us out there." Undisguised glee was visible on Turner's face.

The woman from the stars shrugged, turned the beams on again, raked through the ruins of the nightcreatures once again, rendering them unrecognizable within seconds. "How's that?"

"That will do." Turner faced Oliver. "You ready?"

"As I'll ever be."

"You'll come with us as far as the gates," announced Turner, sweeping a commanding stare over to Anziel. "But *why?*"

"Quite honestly, I don't trust you," replied Turner. "You might laser us in the back to preserve the quaint situation on Styx to further your ambitions. Mightn't you?"

She flushed angrily. "Surely you don't think I'd do *that*. I'm no saint, but neither am I a murderer."

"No. I believe you. But what's to prevent you from stunning us, perhaps, and dragging us back to the ship, depositing our unconscious forms elsewhere, giving Satan a chance to rearm? No, you'll come with us. After these many centuries, I don't wish to take chances."

"He's a maniac!" she said imploringly to Oliver.

"You'd better do what he says," Oliver suggested tonelessly.

"Well, you'd better believe that the stories I'll bring

back of you two will not be complimentary," she said, pivoting from the control board. At the door, she stopped. "Are you coming, or aren't you? I'm pretty sick of this whole world, this whole business, and I want to get *away* from here!"

They stepped through the charred remains of the nightcreatures, made the remaining few yards to the still smoking entrance without trouble.

"I'll go no farther!" Anziel declared as they approached the blasted gates.

"There's no need for you to," the fat man answered without looking at her. "We thank you for your valuable, if somewhat reluctant assistance, Anziel Dubrelicy. You may return to your ship. There's nothing you can do now to hinder or help us."

Oliver watched the woman as she silently strode back to the ship. Whatever else she was, he thought, she was as beautiful as ever. He watched her supple muscles work against the taut fabric of her pants, the graceful sway of her hips.

He would probably never see her again.

A sudden chill wind pounced upon the mountainside, fluttering Anziel's retreating curls, whipping Oliver's shirt as he stood watching her retreat. After waving her bracelet by the forcefield, she stepped up the silver side of her starship, turned, regarded him. But it was too far to read an expression on those lovely features.

"Oliver, if you're coming . . ." Turner clutched the laser pistol in one hand, ready for action.

Oliver unholstered his own, switched the safety off as Anziel had instructed him, and followed Geoffrey Turner into the mouth of Hell.

First there was a corridor, full of silence.

As they entered, the clicks of their boots echoed about them, bouncing off a quiet, faintly lit hall which sliced deep into the mountain.

"Just keep near me," Turner instructed. "It's been half a millennium since I've walked the floors of this place. I'm not entirely sure of the way, but I have my suspicions."

Oliver mutely nodded, his pistol at the ready.

"There's no telling what sort of traps or deadly devices Satan's got rigged in this place now. God knows he's had long enough to prepare it against just such an invasion. So keep close and be ready for anything."

Surprisingly, the danger was a relief for Oliver. The peril swept away the warring thoughts in his mind, strengthened his resolve to offer effective aid to Geoffrey Turner. The adrenalin that surged through him and the eerie silence that raised the hairs on his neck pushed all doubts away for the time being.

A distance down, several corridors intersected.

Turner halted a moment, then came to a decision. "This way, I think."

They turned.

The new corridor was exactly the same as the other: brightly lit; long; sterile. Its sides were gunmetal gray, smooth.

They walked for some time, encountering neither traps nor nightcreatures.

"I can't believe he sent his whole lot out to be slaughtered by Anziel's lasers," Turner murmured. "Nor that we've not encountered further defense . . ."

Abruptly, a thunderous voice blared through the hallway so loud it vibrated Oliver's teeth.

"So, *Turner*. You have finally achieved entrance to Hell."

Turner motioned Oliver to halt. His eyes darted about. "Nicholas?"

"Again, that name," the monotone resounded. "You persist in this fantasy. Well, be that as it may, you *have* achieved something, both you and your companion. You, Turner, are the first Servant of God to have done this. You, Oliver Dolan, are the first mortal."

Turner cocked his head, then seemingly addressed the walls about him. "You still see metal, electronic circuitry, and electricity as items of the spirit, do you

Nicholas? Well, here we are. What do you intend to do about it?"

"It is quite a novel thing for me, Geoffrey Turner, beings of this world descending to Hell of their own accord. I find it most amusing."

"I didn't realize you had a sense of humor."

"Oh, yes. And, just now, it would not amuse me to see you come to your end only partway down my corridor. I am in the mood for guests. You travel the correct way." Bright red arrows began to flash along the sides of the wall. "Just follow these to the elevator, which will take you the rest of the way."

"Why are you being so helpful?" Turner asked suspiciously.

"I have things to discuss with you. And something to show you."

The voice gave way to silence.

"I must say, I thought we'd have to fight our way there."

In silence, they followed the flashing lights. Oliver kept his laser pistol raised, but no nightcreatures pounced, no wall belched fire, no floor fell away to reveal a yawning pit.

At the end of the hall stood the elevator. Its door swished open as they approached.

"Now, as I recall, this lift goes to . . . Ah, yes. Of course . . . to the very *lowest* level of the computer . . . the biomedical section. That is where he'd be if he has grafted himself into the mechanism."

"You mean he's actually giving us an audience without a struggle?" said Oliver, balking at the notion of entering the little compartment Turner had called a lift. The fat man, however, did not hesitate.

"Come, Oliver. I told you the creature was quite mad. I'm sure there's something up his sleeve, but we'll just have to be careful. Meanwhile, the closer we get, the better."

The doors hissed shut, the little compartment began to sink. Oliver noticed that Turner held his gun aimed at the door. He wasn't taking any chances; the boy swerved his pistol there as well.

After a solid minute of descent, the elevator stopped and the doors sighed apart. The stink of sulfur wafted in. Oliver blanched, covered his mouth and nose with his left arm, and squinted against the blur of vermilion and ochre lights shining through tendrils of smoke which coiled from the floor like so many nebulous serpents.

Without hesitation, Turner jounced from the elevator, moved ahead a few yards, then paused to take it all in. Oliver hastened after him. Immediately, the elevator doors snapped shut.

Turner spoke, his words echoing through a vast emptiness. "Some sort of hall, I think. Damned foggy. Smells like hell."

"What now?"

"Advance. Lasers cocked, as it were . . ."

They made their way through scummy smoke which, it seemed to Oliver, parted only reluctantly. In the vague distances were bright, flickering lights—flames, Oliver could see now, rising and falling as though the fringes of the room, or cavern, were afire. The unmarred metal floor occasionally gave way to stretches of craggy rock. Glowing streams of some liquid cut paths here, there, dazzling red in the subdued lighting.

A pillar of flame sprouted suddenly not ten yards from their feet, belching searing heat. The flames writhed like burning tentacles, dancing off the smells of a furnace, twisting about in a high column immediately before them.

From this came a voice, cracking and sibilant, as though the sound itself were aflame: "Far enough for now, my guests. You have arrived in my antechamber. Hark! Hear my welcoming chorus!" A tumult of wails erupted all about them—screams and bloodcurdling yells, cries of agony, breathless howls. "The bodiless souls of the damned who populate this hole," the fire-voice crackled, "who feed my hungers."

Patches of thick smoke were being burned away by

the hot breath of the pillar of flame, revealing a dozen twisted, gnarled demons, their eyes blazing wild reflections. They gamboled about the flames, twisting and writhing in imitation of the flame-tongues, whipping barbed tails against the floor and clicking their hooves in cacophonic beat to unheard music. "My fellows in hell-fire," announced the voice from the pyre. "And now, Geoffrey Turner and Oliver Dolan, welcome. You've come to join us!"

"Not bloody likely!" Turner cried aiming his pistol at the base of the fire-column. "Right, lad? Cut the dancing things to bits." Bright white lanced from Turner's pistol into the base of the fire. Oliver raised his own weapon, pressed the firing stud, and played his beam quickly through the frenzied throng of demons.

An explosion boomed up and out, hurling bits of fiery debris, revealing a metal ceiling not twenty yards above. Oliver's beam brought crackling results, slicing through half the dancers before they realized what was happening, piercing three more as they stopped to shield themselves from the explosion Turner's beam had caused.

The pillar of fire was gone. The remaining demons turned and leaped toward Turner and Oliver, who ripped and slashed them with their beams. The carcasses of the dead things lay sprawled about the floor, mingling their smoke with the returning sulfurous fog.

"No, Nicholas. We're not here to join in on your little fire-parties. We're not here to stay. We've come to stop the source of five hundred years of insanity on this planet. *You!*"

A voice arose again, this time from a far corner of the room. "Has it occurred to you, Turner, that if you fail, I'll not only have gained your deaths, and your souls, but those astonishing weapons as well? Gifts from God, no doubt. And that ship you came in—a fiery chariot. Jehovah has decided to participate hereabouts, it would appear. He can hardly be very intelligent to send so motley a crew against me such as yourselves. But I said I wished to speak to you, and I do.

So please, stay where you are for now. Rest. You'll need your strength. For later."

"Talk!" Turner snarled. "After five centuries, you wish to have a *talk?*"

"Yes. I wish to make you admit that *you* were the one who programed false memories into my system."

"False memories . . . Good Lord, Nicholas . . . you mean to tell me you're beginning to remember how things began here?"

"Yes, I can tell it *was* you. You shall die for this, Turner. Painfully."

"God, man, don't you understand? They're true! You're *not* Satan!"

"I'll hear no more of this—nonsense!" the voice proclaimed. "Now, I said I wished you to see something. I've grown tired of lingering here in my kingdom below. True, I do emerge by means of the senses of my creatures who roam the night. But none of those beings really represent *me!* And so, I have fashioned a body truly befitting my control. One that will strike terror into human hearts. And thus, perhaps I will finally be able to overcome opposition to my total rule of the world!"

And again there was silence. Ominous silence.

"What's he talking about, Geoffrey?"

"Whatever it is, it's not much to my liking. There's no doubt that he brought us here for a reason. And I'm beginning . . . But come. Move off to the side, perhaps we can find a door. I don't like being in the open in this large a space."

Hurriedly, they moved off to the right of the extinguished pillar of flame. "There," Turner said. "Up ahead. I think it's a wall."

Oliver turned to say something, but the words died on his lips. For something—something *huge* seemed to be lumbering toward them from the misty distance. He halted in his tracks, grabbed at Turner's coat, stopping him. "What? Why—?" But Oliver shushed the complaining man, pointed toward the hulk that moved through the smoke.

"What *is* it?" he whispered.

"I don't care to find out right now," Turner said, resuming his speedy retreat. "I just want to find that door."

Deep laughter peeled from hidden speakers. Oliver swiveled his head, only to find that the form bulked nearer, was moving faster. The smoke was clearing. A wind had sprung up from the right side of the vast room, blowing it away. And in the flickering red illumination, Oliver watched the thing that followed as it broke through the retreating haze.

At least thirty feet high from hooves to horns, and proportionately broad, it was a monstrous version of the Satan that Oliver had so often seen in books. Huge bat wings sat on its shoulders. Its legs were those of some gigantic goat. The tail that grew from the hindquarters snaked into a large arrow-shaped barb. The remainder of the beast was modeled after the human form—the torso, the arms, the head. The head wore sharp ears, gleaming horns, and fire-filled eyes.

The horror halted, streaked a clawed hand toward them, pointing. Its mouth opened to reveal razor-sharp fangs.

"Here I am, Turner. My final spiritual body, newly completed. Let us see what you can do against me now!" The words emanated like the roar of a furnace. The thing moved forward.

Turner had long since seen it. He recovered from his initial shock more quickly than Oliver, brought about his gun, and pressed its stud. Burning bright light flicked out to play over the massive creature's chest. But instead of searing flesh, burning circuitry, only a cherry-red spot appeared. And the thing was almost a giant's arm-swipe away.

"The damn thing's all robot!" Turner cried, simultaneously leaping mightily backwards, away from the thing's descending hand.

Oliver dashed around its side, aimed at the face, fired. The part of that face which passed as a cheek glowed red. But there was no harm done to the creature—it directed its gaze downward to Oliver, charged. Dodging around its heavy hooves, he hit the floor, rolled, pushed himself to his feet, than ran forward to the shadowy corner where Turner hid.

"All right, Oliver," said the man, gazing fiercely at the giant swinging back toward them. "One beam won't do it, but perhaps *two* will. The left eye, lad. Quickly."

Obeying, Oliver aimed his sights precisely on the huge pupil of the left eye. Their weapons hummed and the beams intersected in the robot's eye. "Keep it there as long as you can!" cried Turner.

The Satan-monster stepped to the right, but both Oliver and Turner whirled their beams to keep them steady on the eye. The creature raised an arm to protect the eye, but it was too late. Already the hard glass and plastic had given way to the double-power of the lasers; a molten tear streaked down the creature's face.

The thing roared, and immediately turned its back to prevent the blinding of its other eye. Backwards, it dodged toward them.

"We know the weak point!" cried Turner. "Now we've got to get the other one. Separate, move out in front of it. Fry that eye whenever you get the chance."

Turner dashed to the right, Oliver to the left. As soon as they were to the monster's side, Oliver lifted his weapon, beamed the right eye. Turner's laser soon joined it. Again, the giant lifted a protective hand. Again, molten glass and plastic dripped out of a socket.

And with incredible speed, it leaped toward Turner and lashed out blindly. Though the blow glanced off the man, it was powerful enough to hurl him tumbling along the floor. Turner rolled to a stop, and was still.

"Geoffrey!" cried Oliver.

The Satan-thing pivoted toward the new voice, began to move toward it. Realizing his mistake, Oliver reversed course and dashed as silently as possible around the giant to the prostrate Turner. "Are you all right?" he whispered.

"Knocked up a bit," replied Turner. "Can't move—right now." He lifted his right arm slightly. "Quickly.

Take my gun. Keep working at the eyes." In the flicker
of firelight Oliver saw blood welling from the man's
mouth. He grabbed the proffered pistol, gripped it in
his left hand, turned back toward the staggering, sight-
less robot. "That's why he got us down here, in this
room," choked Turner. "Thought this thing would be
invulnerable to the lasers. Show him that's not the
case, lad."

Oliver nodded.

Turner's voice had risen to a croak, attracting the
Satan-robot's attention. It swerved and headed toward
them. Taking aim with both guns, Oliver unleashed
their energy upon the right eye-socket. His aim with
the left pistol was faulty; he adjusted it, pulsing all the
light-energy of the guns into the beast's eyeless hole.
Smoke began to curl from the socket.

The giant halted, brought up its hand to shield the
vulnerable socket, then renewed its advance. Hardly
thinking, Oliver ran to obtain a different angle, and
let loose with the beams again. This time he was rewarded with a crackle, a gout of fire from the eye-hole
before it was again shielded. The monster put its left
arm up against its face, kept it there. Oliver lowered
the beams, played them into the open mouth which
gnashed closed, but not before a hole was burned in
its roof.

The huge tail whistled around, seeking to strike him.
Oliver backed away, then ran. He had noticed that each
of the giant's faculties seemed to correspond to human
faculties: it saw through eyes, spoke through a mouth—
therefore, it must hear through its ears. Oliver aimed
at one of those cavities, fired, kept the beams on it as
long as he dared, then leapt from a slash of the thing's
right claws. The creatures, sensing an opportunity,
smashed down with its left arm, just missing the breathless boy. But this time, instead of running, Oliver stood
fast, took aim, and fired into the socket of the right
eye once again.

Suddenly the thing froze.

Wary of a trick, Oliver kept the lasers trained on

the eye. Sparks jumped, flames spouted, smoke poured from the eyes, the nose, the mouth.

Satisfied that he had halted the thing, Oliver ran back to Turner, who had propped himself up on his hands.

"Good show, Oliver. You've burned out the wireless link to Satan's command center. Now, help me to my feet: I know where that command center must be."

Leaning on Oliver for support, Turner eventually located the passageway.

It angled deeper and at its end was the deepest chamber of Hell, where the living creature that was Satan lived.

This was even more hell-like, Oliver noted, than the antechamber.

Its only occupant was the pitiful thing in the nutrient bath. They walked up to it. It spoke.

"Your weapons of light have been your salvation," the voice intoned from hanging speakers. "And yet, I think they will not kill *me*."

Turner limped forward, shrugging off Oliver's aid. "And what makes you think that, Nicholas? God, you're a terrible sight, man!" Turner's side was bloody where the devil had struck. His voice was weak.

"The decripit body you see before you is only a tool, Turner, a vessel of my Plan. Soon my consciousness shall be totally of my spiritual self, buried within this mountain. It shall be me, and I it. As for why you will not kill me—*this* is why!"

A dozen demons rained down on them from the ceiling. They dropped onto Turner and Oliver, knocking their lasers to the floor, holding them fast. Oliver struggled, but it was hopeless. Turner fought valiantly, but the things clawed and gashed him unmercifully.

"Hold!" Satan commanded. "Do not finish him yet."

Geoffrey Turner was in sad shape. The demons had ripped off his shirt, torn his chest. His electronic circuitry was exposed. But he still breathed. He was yet conscious.

"You have won, Satan," he said, bloody spittle running down his chin. "I came close, but you have won. I give up. My soul is yours."

"You are a realist. I can see that," said the voice from the speakers. "You have been a worthy opponent these past centuries. But it was your destiny to come to this. Fate is on my side."

"You are correct."

"Geoffrey!" Oliver cried. "Don't give in *now!*" He struggled fiercely with his captors but to no avail. Their strength was inhuman.

Turner's voice croaked louder: "But Nicholas—or, rather, Satan. You claim this body of the person we know to be Hedley Nicholas, in the nutrient tank before me, is only a tool. That your consciousness is now entirely in your machine—I mean, spiritual self. That would explain much."

"What do you mean, Turner?"

"I mean that those troublesome memories stored within you—those *human* memories—are those of this wreck of a man in the nutrient bath, Hedley Nicholas. The vessel of flesh that carried your profound spirit to this planet. Those memories are not *yours,* Satan. In the past centuries, you have merely been using this wasted creature's body as a crutch. Tell me. Can you see through this man's eyes as well as your other creatures' eyes? What *function* is this—this piece of fleshly junk you've stored here? Why, none at all now, if what you tell me is true."

"You mouth conclusions I have already arrived at, Turner. Thank you. But what are you getting at?"

"I'm dying, Satan. I can feel that. And yet I find myself totally awed by your magnificence, your grandeur. I would that I could *serve* you."

"But as you say, you are dying. How can you serve me?"

"You have totally absorbed the faculties of this creature by now. This Hedley Nicholas is of no further use to you. Why not disconnect this parasite. Why not slough him off, and attach yourself to *me?* Absorb *my* faculties. The tank will keep me alive long enough for that, surely."

There was silence.

Oliver gazed at Turner, wide-eyed. What was the meaning of all this? He wanted to say something, but he found himself speechless.

"You *do* have much to offer. Much knowledge," Satan said finally.

"And that knowledge will become your knowledge, Satan. Discard this worthless hulk in the tank. *He* is Hedley Nicholas. *He* was merely a carrier of your consciousness. *He* is the cause of all your self-doubts."

Incredibly, the tank-being's eyes bulged larger.

"No!" said the voice from the speakers. "*I* am Satan. I, in the tank."

"No," countered an echo of the same voice. "I, in the machine, am Satan. You are my servant!"

"But I *control* the machine!" the garbled voice said. "It is my spiritual body." The thing in the tank seemed to gurgle.

Suddenly, Oliver felt the strong grips of the demons slacken. The body in the tank suffered convulsions as the voice from the speaker warred with itself, squealing and buzzing with feedback. Oliver pulled away from the demons that held him—and they did not try to stop him.

Free, he looked over to Turner. The fat man had fallen and lay bleeding on the floor. All the creatures in the chamber were still. The liquid in the bath spilled over the tank walls as the thing Turner had called Hedley Nicholas squirmed within it.

"Quickly, Oliver," choked Turner. "Destroy him while you've the chance!"

Shocked from his momentary paralysis, Oliver searched about for his gun, found it, scooped it up.

He aimed at the tank-creature's head.

Its eyes bulged. The speakers had time to say "No!" before the beam spurted from the weapon's nozzle, slicing off its head.

Bright red blood turned the tank crimson.

The speakers frizzled off.

Oliver turned to protect himself from the demons. But they were still as statues, their horrible forms frozen.

His breaths coming quick and heavy, Oliver scanned the chamber for other dangers. He recognized none.

It was over; all over, so quickly. He could not believe it.

"Well, lad," Turner said from the floor. "We've done it." But there was no joy in the voice, no triumph. Only pain.

He was lying belly down, the side of his face pressed against the cold metal floor.

Oliver walked over, knelt down by him, laser pistol still dangling in his limp hand. "You mean *you've* done it, Geoffrey. You deserve the credit, not me. How— *what* did you do?"

"Credit?" A chuckle wracked the man's form. "There's no credit here. Just a duty. Just a duty." His eyes rolled up to Oliver. "It was the last hope, really. I could tell from the session with Nicholas via telecommunication at Lord Billington's that the man was fairly upset. It was his schizophrenia. He didn't know for sure whether he was in the machine, or in that body. It was hard for him to accept the fact anymore that he was in the body, because I proved to him that that was Hedley Nicholas' body. And yet, part of him *knew* that if he disconnected that body, it would be suicide. So an interior battle was fought there, which focused attention away from us, giving you one more chance. Which you took, quite splendidly."

"What . . . what can I do? Surely if this is a medical wing—and the computer still functions, I can see that you're healed."

"No," Turner said in a garbled voice. He shook his head loosely. "It's too late for that, now. The computer's probably in a state of dormancy now. Besides, even if you could, I wouldn't want you to."

"But . . . why? It's just coming to me now . . . there's no more Satan, Geoffrey. No more Nightworld. All the nightcreatures must be as still as these are—they'll just die! Styx is free! All your goals have been accomplished. This world will be a paradise again."

"You really think so, Oliver? No. Not likely. Anziel will take back news of us. Dozens of spacecraft will be here in a few months, to change our way of life. You know, it's ironic. Poor Nicholas did more to keep the lifestyle here static than anything else. Perhaps, if we'd not been fighting him, we'd have been fighting ourselves." He closed his eyes. "I want nothing to do with Anziel's lot. I know that now."

He laughed quietly. "It's funny, Oliver. The man that I was modeled after was a seer who looked into the future, a man I know quite well, for I almost *was* him for a while. But I've changed over the years, lad. Oh God, I've changed. I'm my own person, whoever that is. And feel damned proud to have lived and served an ideal of the past, as impossibly foolish as it might have been. Because, Oliver, the Empire *meant* something. It gave life some *purpose*. I've fulfilled my purpose, now. Satan is destroyed. To go on living would be meaningless."

"But just to *live*. To *survive*. Is that not purpose enough, Geoffrey?"

"For a tree, perhaps. Or a deer, a mouse, a bird. But for a thinking individual, Oliver?" He shook his head weakly. "No. It's *not* enough."

He pushed his hand out, and Oliver took that hand, squeezed it warmly. "Geoffrey?"

But the pulse in the hand had stopped.

EPILOGUE

WHEN he found his way out of the mountain's depths, it was yet dark.

The starship remained in the valley.

No forcefield surrounded the vessel. As he strode past, its entrance slid open, the ramp angled out. Light spilled through—a rosy illumination half-blocked by the figure of a woman.

"You're safe," she said. About her torso she wore a skin-tight glossy sheath ornamented with strips of dazzling, winking lights and gemstone clusters. This material rose to a point just below her breasts, which were bare beneath the translucence of a silky top. Her legs were wrapped in the gauzy nothing of a full, sweeping skirt speckled with mirror-beads that shone in the light.

"I've waited for you, Oliver."

She tossed her sleek head back majestically. Her

hair streamed up in a cloud of curling strands above her. The cool backlighting made a nimbus of it, a corona around the bright-sun beauty that was her face. She stared expectantly at him.

"Thanks for the use of your weapons," he said bitterly. He tossed the laser pistols her way. She moved smoothly aside; the guns banged onto the floor behind her.

"Where is Turner?" she asked softly.

"Dead."

"And Satan?"

"Destroyed."

"Ah. So much for my plans for this world." She looked up at the stars absently. "No matter. This will be an interesting enough discovery, this Styx. I will have my story. A parcel of fame will be mine." She gazed at him searchingly. "And it can be yours as well, Oliver."

She stepped down gracefully, wafted toward him, hair and dress streaming dreamily behind, caught up with moonbeams. She slid slim arms about his smoke-smudged body. She smelled of a hundred varieties of sweet flowers mixed subtly, delicately.

"Two nights ago, I told you to think about the stars, Oliver," she breathed. Her soft tones caressed his ear. She nibbled a tingly kiss onto the lobe. "The stars are yours if you'll come with me. They're yours, if you're mine. And you'll see, feel, sense a thousand new things, Oliver. No, more. I have much to offer." She looked at him coyly. "Not least among which is myself."

His arms rose. He embraced her enticing smoothness. He held her for some time. Then he let her go, turned away.

"You're not angry with me, are you?" she purred demurely.

"No. There is no reason to be," he replied. "You can only be what you are."

She stepped around, touched his chin, smiled glowingly. "Then you'll come home with me?"

"No."

Her expression revealed perplexity. "But why?"

"I admit that to come with you, and thus expand my universe, would be the next logical step."

She cocked her head. "I sense . . . a difference in you."

"Do you?"

She nodded. "You are attracted to me, by what I have to offer?"

"Yes."

"Oh, Oliver! Then *abandon* this little *nothing* of an antiquated world. There is so much potential in you. Don't *waste* it here. I have so much to offer. Do you think I'd have waited if I didn't care for you? Of course not. I don't understand why, but I do. Self-sufficient, independent Anziel Dubrelicy, in love! My father would have a *fit* of laughter.

"I was going to take off as soon as possible. But I couldn't. God, it was all I could do to keep myself from going in after you."

Oliver looked away from her beauty, breathed deeply, stared out at the forest.

"This is my world, Anziel," he said. "This is my home. All you offer me is empty. Your universe echoes with emptiness, Anziel. It is too vast, too huge for my comprehension. I can't tell you the struggle my mind has gone through in the past week. My small, comfortable world exploded into infinity. I've tasted eternity, Anziel, I've had a touch of space and time, of reality, and I find it very chill, inhospitable.

"This universe I've found is mad. Now I even find the events of this 'noble' quest absurd—any meaning it might have had died with Geoffrey Turner. There's no sense to our immediate existence. No sense but what each individual makes for himself." He looked up at her. "No rhyme or reason except for poems, Anziel. Poems I must write for myself." He paused. "Do you have a religion?"

"No. I believe . . . well, I suppose I believe in progress, in mankind. I really haven't given it much thought."

"You don't believe in a God?"

"Never did. It's not fashionable."

"Well, Anziel, this past week I *lost* a God. And I can't tell you what a void that leaves in me. It hurts. I feel sick. But I know now that it is a necessary pain. My God was too small. A puny, anthropomorphized deity, full of false mystery and nonsense verse. He was *my* God, I clutched at him in a frenzy—and he vanished. No. None of us can own God, and call him ours. But He's there. He has to be, or the common denominator of all life is emptiness, nothingness, and I can't accept that. No, the God I owned was drilled into me. I never looked for him, for I thought he was all around me, and the forces of his opposition were the night-creatures."

"I don't understand," she said.

"I still have that void in me, Anziel. I know it would be foolish to fill it with myself, as I'd do if I indulged in your universe, as much as I care to.

"No. I've made my choice. The people of this world are going to be baffled when they find themselves free of 'Satanic' forces. The parameters of society will dissolve, the boundaries will crumble. I must stay here and do what I can. I must remain, to find new hope for my people, and myself. I must prepare them for the coming of *your* civilization. I must enlarge their vision of God. And my own vision.

"This is my choice." He looked into her eyes. "Perhaps you could return, stay with me. I've nothing to offer, though. I'm not even sure I love you."

She was frowning. "You're a fool, Oliver Dolan."

He shook his head. "No. Not anymore. Not anymore."

Not even looking back, she stormed away, and entered her ship.

After a while, it floated up into the sky. Oliver watched the comet-like streak bloom and fade into the night sky. He walked into the forest. For the first time, he had no fear of the night that surrounded him.

Leaning determinedly into a new-risen and bitter wind, he strode into the cold Nightworld, the now-harmless Nightworld, toward the horizon from which the sun would rise.

ABOUT THE AUTHOR

David Bischoff was born December 15, 1951, in Washington, D.C. Long a resident of Maryland, David earned his B.A. (1973) in Radio, TV, and Film at the University of Maryland. He lives in Adelphi, single with no pets, a full-time writer.

To help ends meet he holds down a part-time position at NBC Washington and teaches occasional writing courses for local colleges.

A science-fiction fan since his early teens, Mr. Bischoff has been active in local and national sf functions. He is presently Secretary for the Science Fiction Writers of America.

His passions, besides science fiction, include British Television, film, and European rock music.

Although he has produced many short stories and several collaborative novels, *Nightworld* is his first solo novel.

Jack L. Chalker

A JUNGLE OF STARS	25457	1.50
THE WEB OF THE CHOZEN	27376	1.75
MIDNIGHT AT THE WELL OF SOULS	25768	1.95
DANCERS IN THE AFTERGLOW	27564	1.75

James P. Hogan

INHERIT THE STARS	25704	1.50
THE GENESIS MACHINE	27231	1.75
THE GENTLE GIANTS OF GANYMEDE	27375	1.75

Tony Rothman

THE WORLD IS ROUND	27213	1.95

DEL REY SCIENCE FICTION CLASSICS FROM BALLANTINE BOOKS

CHILDHOOD'S END,
Arthur C. Clarke 27603 1.95
FAHRENHEIT 451, Ray Bradbury 27431 1.95
HAVE SPACESUIT, WILL TRAVEL,
Robert A. Heinlein 26071 1.75
IMPERIAL EARTH, Arthur C. Clarke 25352 1.95
MORE THAN HUMAN,
Theodore Sturgeon 24389 1.50
RENDEZVOUS WITH RAMA,
Arthur C. Clarke 27344 1.95
RINGWORLD, Larry Niven 27550 1.95
A SCANNER DARKLY,
Philip K. Dick 26064 1.95
SPLINTER OF THE MIND'S EYE,
Alan Dean Foster 26062 1.95
STAND ON ZANZIBAR,
John Brunner 25486 1.95
STAR WARS, George Lucas 26079 1.95
STARMAN JONES,
Robert A. Heinlein 27595 1.75
TUNNEL IN THE SKY,
Robert A. Heinlein 26065 1.50
UNDER PRESSURE, Frank Herbert 27540 1.75